EVENT HORIZON

EVENT HORIZON

BALSAM KARAM

Translated from the Swedish by Saskia Vogel

THE FEMINIST PRESS
AT THE CITY UNIVERSITY OF NEW YORK
NEW YORK CITY

Published in 2026 by the Feminist Press
at the City University of New York
The Graduate Center
365 Fifth Avenue, Suite 6200
New York, NY 10016

feministpress.org

First Feminist Press edition 2026

Händelsehorisonten by Balsam Karam was first published in 2018 by Norstedts, Sweden

This book is made possible by the New York State Council on the Arts with the support of the Office of the Governor and the New York State Legislature.

First printing March 2026

Cover design by Sara R. Acedo
Text design by Drew Stevens

Library of Congress Cataloging-in-Publication Data
Names: Karam, Balsam author | Vogel, Saskia translator
Title: Event horizon / Balsam Karam ; translated from the Swedish by Saskia Vogel.

Description: First Feminist Press edition. | New York City : Feminist Press at the City University of New York, 2026.
Identifiers: LCCN 2025049249 (print) | LCCN 2025049250 (ebook) | ISBN 9781558613546 paperback | ISBN 9781558613553 ebook
Subjects: LCGFT: Science fiction | Novels | Fiction
Classification: LCC PT9877.21.A725 H3613 2026 (print) | LCC PT9877.21.A725 (ebook)
LC record available at https://lccn.loc.gov/2025049249
LC ebook record available at https://lccn.loc.gov/2025049250

PRINTED IN THE UNITED STATES OF AMERICA

To my beloved daughters
Havana Prince Karam
Evora Farah Havana Karam

Beloved
You are my sister
You are my daughter
You are my face; you are me
—Toni Morrison

As to all the talk about how Marcos is homosexual: Marcos is gay in San Francisco, black in South Africa, Asian in Europe, Chicano in San Ysidro, an anarchist in Spain, Palestinian in Israel, Mayan Indian in the streets of San Cristóbal, a gang member in Neza, a punk at university, a Jew in Germany, an ombudsman in the military, a feminist in the political parties, a communist in the post–Cold War, a prisoner in Cintalapa Prison, a pacifist in Bosnia, Mapuche in the Andes, a teacher in the CNTE, an artist without a gallery or portfolio, a housewife on a Saturday night in any neighborhood in any Mexico there is, a guerrilla in late twentieth-century Mexico, a person striking at the CTM, an honest reporter in the domestic newsroom, a machista in the feminist movement, a woman alone on the subway at ten o'clock at night, a pensioner in a demonstration on Zócalo Square, a smallholder farmer without land, a marginalized editor, an unemployed worker, a doctor without a post, a rebellious student, a dissident under neoliberalism, an author without books and readers, and, what is certain, a Zapatista in southeastern Mexico. Marcos is a human being like any other in this world. Marcos is all oppressed minorities when they resist, explode and say 'Ya Basta!' All the oppressed as they search for a word, their word, that which gives back the majority to those eternally fragmented, us.

—Subcomandante Marcos

PROLOGUE

ON EARTH IN A place like any other, where a gridded city reached for the sea with wide beaches that sometimes repelled the sea and sometimes invited it in, one of the mothers of the Outskirts had been kneeling in the lantern light on the boardwalk, pushing a bicycle chain into place.

As always at night, she'd just risen from the ground any ground and shaken the sand and shells from her sweater—the starry sky black and infinite had revealed itself and her finger had followed Ursa Major towards Orion and Ursa Minor and onward to Gemini and Virgo and stopped at Venus, bigger and brighter than ever before.

She studied the stars in the sky and in the flashlight light made careful notes on the span of the sky and the celestial bodies' activities on this night, first noting the date and time then recording every difference from the previous night worth recording (not many) and divining the conditions for tomorrow night (very good) and what the stars were saying on the whole about the state of the world as it was right that moment (surprisingly much).

Soon the glittering gold notebook Essa had given her was full and once again she'd have to carry off white paper bags from shops in town and, in the light of the only lantern in the Outskirts, measure, cut and bind her own notebooks to have with her wherever she went. Every birthday she asked Essa how she'd been able to afford this, and every year Essa answered with only a kiss and two cups of hot coffee for them to take to the slope in the afternoon light, sitting down where the bushes along the slope thickened just as the sky raised the mist above the Outskirts and let it fall into twilight.

Here at the boardwalk, the sky was still bright with stars and the road leading out empty and smooth. She tucked her notebook away and picked up a full bicycle basket from the sand, pedalling slowly as she set off along the road, polishing as she went the fruits—found in trash cans around the city—to a gleam against her sweater now in tatters across her body. She nibbled the ripe plums she'd pinched from the greengrocer's stand that she'd once owned and thought warm thoughts of Pepe and his cart.

Maybe Pepe had noticed her walking around the stand, from one side to the other, earlier in the day right as the afternoon crowd grew denser and bag after bag was held out to him for weighing and payment; maybe he'd flinched when she, having snuck around the watermelons and rutabagas, suddenly appeared in line with the ears of corn ten for two and plums both yellow and pink; maybe he'd wanted to say something but stopped himself, not sure if she wanted to be seen or intended to come and go unnoticed. She'd been sneaking, that much was true, but she wasn't ashamed of what she was doing; there was no shame in taking what you needed, and besides, who but Pepe would let her help herself to the earth's bounty, just like she had offered him that one day when it was still her stand? Here you go, is what she'd said, arms outstretched as if in an embrace, and Pepe had watched as she turned and like now began to make her slow way to the Outskirts.

Early summer, the jasmine shrubs in bloom along the streets leading out of the city. This mother of the Outskirts, once a greengrocer, was now on her way home to those she loved and who loved her back, and everywhere she felt as if from the warming world to the embracing trees and everything in between she was wished well. The rats that had spent the day hiding from white tourist feet crept carefully along the road, and struck by tenderness, she tossed them two soft tomatoes and her half-eaten plum. Take it, she said quietly and cycled on, enjoy.

She wasn't aware of this, but later that same night she'd be the last of the mothers to see Milde alive as she cycled past the disused execution site and noticed it was illuminated.

During the day, the nooses hung high enough to catch the eyes of passersby when a gust sent them swaying over the wall, but now—just as the sun was beginning to rise—two of the four floodlights were on and a white van was parked outside.

The greengrocer stopped, leaned her bike against the wall, climbed onto the saddle to take a look.

There was a woman, young, gaunt. Surrounded by two white men and another two beside. She had short hair and an eye patch, hands tied behind her back.

One of the men, a boy, tore off the patch and handed it to the other. He addressed her, waited for a reply. She replied, but what did she say? Impossible to hear and soon the exchange was over.

The boy fitted a dark cloth over the woman's head and took off her slippers. He led her to the noose, white as chalk, and the woman held her head high as it was tightened.

All was early summer yet, and now—as before—the jasmine was jasmine and the sky was streaked blue-green and every dawn henceforth was bound to this.

From that place came no sound other than the men's voices as this mother once greengrocer climbed down from the saddle and rushed away from there.

Later, when a courier delivered to Essa a cardboard box, crammed at the bottom of which were her daughter Milde's few belongings, the mother once greengrocer upon seeing the eye patch realized at once who that young woman had been. The mothers and children of the Outskirts would set off that same night for the city, down the slope and onto the highway, past the gas stations and in among the whitewashed houses that marked the beginning and end of the city. In groups and lines through the city, two by two or four by four, like a scattered then gathered string of pearls, the mothers and children of the Outskirts would walk, letting every burning car become a lantern and every hurled stone a song; along the boardwalk that the children had so often walked with a cooler on their arm or a rake in hand were now burning piles of sun loungers and trash cans overturned on the street; along the avenues where the children had dragged their cut-up feet, the mothers now walked, stopping at every café and restaurant, asking people to get up, to join them. The children and mothers cried out for no rest, no peace until the Outskirts that Milde loved and that loved her back was informed of what had become of her, but no news came and no Milde returned home.

As if hunted, the greengrocer would set off through the sugarcane fields sharp against her bare feet and continue up to the mountains where glowing red they towered in the east. She would climb to the steppe and into the half-desert, on up to the caves that offered cool relief and peace. Once there, surrounded by rock and dust, she would seek out the place where her hero Milde had once been in hiding and would herself lie down.

Back then—when no one but Milde was being searched for and no one else was accused of setting the fire that had spread in the heat from the city planning office to the Ministry of Education and on to the embassies next door—the Outskirts had collected the coins from every sold beach ball, towel and ceramic necklace and bought Milde all the tins and bottles of water she could carry. They'd asked her to be as careful as could be and told her that she'd be checked on from time to time, be given everything she needed from time to time—but she had to understand that it was of the utmost importance that she stay in hiding and not get ideas about returning home, Do you hear me? Not for a while, Essa had pleaded, as she packed her daughter's bag—Don't come home for a few months, Essa had said turning to Milde, who nodded and promised without hesitation, Yes, absolutely, a few months, no problem.

There, perhaps leaning against the same wall, the mother once greengrocer would sit for two days and three nights, neither eating food nor drinking water, sleeping only when the sun was beating white and large against the cave walls and the ammonia of evaporating urine rose towards her face.

By the time the mother once greengrocer returned to the Outskirts, a story had taken shape in her mind, and she stuck to it when she began to write.

So it was and so it went, she wrote—such was Milde and such was her eternal life.

MILDE IS SEVENTEEN YEARS old and has just reached the mouth of the cave. There are no carvings on the walls and ground, only droppings and dust. She picks up a pellet, puts it to her nose, tries to guess from which animal it came but can't tell. Lizard shit? Hard to say.

Milde pulls the shawl off her shoulders and spreads it out on the ground where she will sit, eat, sleep and stand—she beats the shawl against the walls to release its dust then spreads it out again and again on the ground.

She wants to wet the ground to settle the dust but can't spare the water. She drinks, convinces herself that she need only rinse her face and hands at the end of the day, so she washes where she wants to make her bed. The water runs over her head, neck and breasts and onto the cave floor, and in this way Milde gets her dampened ground. Well done, clever, she thinks and sits down, and after that she's at a loss.

It is the month of May, and a few nights ago in the city's dark, Milde set two buildings on fire. The third, where there was a guard on site who saw and could describe Milde, caught fire by chance. The fault of the wind, the trees, she doesn't know. She lies down and thinks about the guard who saw her, how surprised he seemed to be. Then she thinks of all the mothers and children of the Outskirts and falls asleep.

MILDE, ASTRONAUT FROM THE OUTSKIRTS

ON EARTH IN A place like any other, where a gridded city reached for the sea with wide beaches that sometimes repelled the sea and sometimes invited it in, a greengrocer stood bent over herself and the fruit she'd harvested, polishing tomato after tomato to a gleam on her shirt. She picked flies out of the pile of romaine lettuce beside the tomatoes and cleared the weeds and blossoms from the cilantro.

Morning, a town square. A buzz rose from the place, lush and soft, and around the streets, the blossoming jasmine burst into scent, asserting itself. Under the trees cats lay in clusters and along the avenues waiters would soon be serving white tourists their first cups of coffee and later glasses of red wine, on the beach some would eagerly undress and dive in, and through the schoolyards the bells would soon resound.

Shortly the square would fill with older folks who'd finished their morning tea but had yet to start on lunch. Wearing flimsy sun visors and tops in pale colors, they would cross the square, greeting the greengrocer at her stand, taking a seat on the park benches to the right of the library and each taking out their own crumpled pack of cigarettes. While they were sneaking a smoke in the shade of the cherry trees, occasionally exchanging a few words, the greengrocer would step forward with a peach for each of them and accept a bunch of cigarettes in return. She'd smoke two right away and say, Thank you, bye, slowly return to her stand and look out over the square.

Night and the night's starry sky longed for by the greengrocer was still far off—another ten hours at the stand and then an hour or so of cleaning and after that the walk home. She would pull her cart down the cobbled streets to the buildings almost in ruins and to the blue door which, for want of anything else, she'd closed with a hook; from there she would manoeuvre the cart as best she could down the long, narrow corridor and once within the courtyard park it against a wall and sit. Eventually she'd muster the energy to kick off the shoes she'd been wearing all day and fold out the mattress she'd hidden from the early summer rain that sometimes surprised the city in the afternoon, stopping as suddenly as it started. She would lie on her back in the middle of the courtyard and gaze at the starry sky vast and endlessly beautiful.

On the floor above, close enough for the girl

to catch the plums the greengrocer tossed up to her, a family had once lived. After the roof collapsed one morning, just as the children had finished packing their school bags and were ready to go, the family decided to move two blocks over to another condemned building almost as nice as any other building, almost as clean and orderly. Our rent will go up quite a bit, but we'll just have to grit our teeth, said the mother, looking up from her packing. We can't live like this, afraid of walls caving in, what kind of life is that? The two of us will have to work twice as much, but if we shut off the electricity and hot water, we'll manage. Won't you be moving too, the mother had asked, hoping for a yes. The greengrocer, who was unpacking her cart at the time, had nodded kindly and taken the mother in her arms, filled a bag from what remained on the cart and followed the family through the streets to the new building almost as good as any proper building and almost as orderly. As for the greengrocer, she was happy that the hot weather would soon be on its way and that the night's sleep would be pleasant once more. At night she dreamed of the sea and during the day she longed for the night and the starry sky, and was happy for the vision of the night and the starry sky, even when she could not bring herself to conjure them.

She wrote in her notebook that she was happy that even this late in life the apparition of night brought joy and longing to her body, that feelings such as joy and longing still had a place in her broken body. My body, she wrote, is in disrepair. But now the apparition of night is here and now it is playing within me as joy; now as the morning sun is sweeping across the city and has the cafés carrying out chairs and tablecloths and now as the waiters line up lunch menus and chill aperitifs.

In the mornings where the vegetable stand stood, its back to the tailor's, first the taxi drivers passed by and then those who'd travelled from far to work construction. The greengrocer greeted them all and sat down on a stool, kept hidden behind baskets of sweet cherries and apples and which she'd occasionally take out to rest her swollen legs on, dark veins already apparent. From time to time, she would get up to dip a towel in the fountain's warm water to cool her neck with, then would return to her seat and go back to stacking the fruit and vegetables.

The mother once greengrocer was a year or so younger than Essa but older than Milde would ever get to be; she knew the Outskirts well but couldn't have imagined that Milde from the Outskirts would be crossing the square on this morning.

Back when she was a greengrocer she'd stood at the foot of the Outskirts many times and was invited in, drank tea with the mothers and children and talked to them about the uprising, said she thought that the uprising was brave and correct and something had to be done about the situation—that the only person who'd had the courage to talk about it all had been Milde and it was still incomprehensible that her punishment had been so grave, so harsh. A seventeen-year-old, a child who'd spoken like a thousand leaders during her own trial! No, it wasn't right, she'd only said and done what no one else had dared, isn't that right? Had she not lent her voice to all who for years had kept their mouths shut out of fear? Had she not said what needed to be said, about how we've been treated and how one day it must end?

The mothers had nodded and tried to remember Milde's face just before she had to leave for the cave, and the children who'd sat tensely at their sides listening to the greengrocer had looked at their mothers and waited for more. Afterwards the greengrocer was given more tea and her own private tour of the homes, each one of thin but sturdy metal walls worn by a love she couldn't describe at the time because she had yet to experience it. She'd stepped out of one of the homes, glass of tea in hand, and sat with her back against the cool metal wall, feeling welcome somewhere for the first time in a very long time, and then and there decided to stay the night.

The greengrocer had only seen Milde in the photos and newspaper clippings that Essa always carried with her and couldn't possibly have recognized her. The uprising had taken place eleven years ago and besides, these eyes weren't what they should have been, cloudy and misty and not one bit as sharp as they should have been.

The greengrocer hadn't recognized Milde on that morning and later couldn't forgive herself for it. Shortly after Milde's departure for the black hole called the Mass, the greengrocer left the city, packed what little she could carry and moved in with Essa at the heart of the Outskirts.

On that morning, the greengrocer had gotten up from her stool, done the weighing and taken payment, put out and put away, occasionally exchanging a few words with acquaintances who raised their hands in greeting as they passed by. It was going to be a hot day, you could tell, and billowing in the slender shadows of the trees that framed the square to the east and west, the cigarette smoke continued to rise among the cherry blossoms soon fallen to the ground, lingering there like fog or haze. Still morning, one of the older folks would set their book in someone else's hands and stub out their cigarette against the sole of their shoe—another would wipe their forehead with their visor then put it back on.

Today the buzz in the square was loud and the greengrocer would later recall that the whole square had been awake.

On a square like any other—lined by a fish restaurant, a tailor's shop, two public toilets and a library—two policemen and yet another white man crossed the carved stone slabs. They had a woman with them.

The greengrocer looked on as they came walking—looked at the woman and sought her gaze—but still did not recognize her.

Of the four, the woman was the most gaunt but also the most striking; she moved like a carp, black clad, hair cut short, passing children who turned to look at her folded trouser hems and large loose shirt, her black cloth bag softly draping her shoulder and her face scarred from eye to cheek.

How old was she? What was she doing there?

The greengrocer would later write: Still early in the summer the sun driving hard on the place, brightening; still morning a gentle breeze cooled arms and legs, and the sand spread on the square was whipped up once more to a flurry, whisked from bench to bush and back, moving like clouds towards the beach where the white children, among the summer's first tourists, joined in on each other's howls and stood up, volleying beach balls and giggling.

Soon someone would fill a bucket with water to be carried with care, cross the square and the flagstones and splash water on the sand so it would settle and a cool scent arise. Like a victory rush the coolness would then sweep through the square and in gusts reach the greengrocer's stand and the basketseller sleepy in the shade.

The coolness would also reach the striking woman who at that moment stopped, looked around, shut her eyes. It was the month of May, just before noon on a Tuesday, and just when the policemen moved to shove Milde onward, she would herself turn around and keep going.

In the library where, under police surveillance, the astronomer and Milde had entered, the intended experiment was like a lit candle placed on the white table before them—flickering nameless and impatiently waiting to speak.

On the table was a large jug of cold water and a bowl of ripe peaches that the greengrocer had picked out and been paid for. Later, when she'd realized that the woman crossing the square wasn't just anybody, but the Milde who was *the* Milde—the one the greengrocer had always wanted to meet, embrace and praise—the greengrocer would wish that she'd either sold nothing at all to that astronomer or sold the finest peaches in her peach pyramid, which she was constantly depleting and rebuilding.

This is what she would have wished for, and she'd long wondered whether Milde had even taken a bite of peach.

Later, she would decide that Milde had indeed taken a peach but that she must have set the peach sun-ripe and deep yellow aside in anticipation of the meeting being over. The greengrocer couldn't imagine Milde tucking into the fruit in the company of those white men—no, ugh, impossible—but did spend a while toying with the idea of how Milde might later in the back seat of the police car have eaten the greengrocer's fruit in peace and quiet and for the last time ever looked out over the city she'd never loved anyway, except for the fact that somewhere it contained the Outskirts.

Yes, so it must have been, wrote the greengrocer, and while the meeting was going on, Milde, as the only civilized human being sitting around that white table, had clasped her hands in her lap and waited.

The astronomers around the table, papers stacked in front of them, looked around the room expectantly, nodded at Milde, showed her to an empty chair. Milde sat down and said hello, her voice deep but no particular darkness to her tone and her body slightly leaned back. One of the men poured water and as the peach bowl went around the table Milde chose the finest peach she'd ever seen and set it aside.

One of the astronomers said: Now yet another mass has disappeared, does anyone know where it might have gone?

Another cleared their throat and said: I wonder, is it possible for mass to disappear and never be found again? Have you ever had a pocket in which keys weighed down by a medallion large and midnight blue—a gift from a distant relative or lover travelling across the seas—have sunk to a depth exceeding the length of your pants, beyond even the floor and all the floors below, beyond the ground, beyond everything above and below?

The experiment, now brought to life, shook its light across the table and called attention to itself, began to speak. It said: Do you know about the black hole called the Mass? There you will find what does not want to be found but exists nonetheless.

The experiment, now wide awake, continued: I have long known about the Mass and what it conceals—dreamed of how it draws all other masses to it and claims them. I have long known about the Mass, known that it's approaching; it's there at the threshold, waiting, lurking, longing. I'm now looking for a body that wants to get to know the Mass as I have always wanted to without knowing how. A body that wants to filter the feeling of an incomparable depth and a place completely surrounded by itself—a body that endures a loneliness lacking rightful designation and knows that such an experience can neither be shared nor explained. I wish for that body to be by my side and at the same time I want it to know that what I'm asking for is immense.

I wonder, the experiment said, still flickering but as reborn above the earth, is there one such body around this table?

The experiment went on: I'm talking about big steps, for mankind, for the body that is able to picture itself stepping into bottomlessness and for the world that will come to observe the event from afar.

What I'm asking means never being able to be buried or return to the home where the smell of bird cherry on an early summer evening mingles with that of scorched earth and garbage, and never being able to stand by the fire—making coffee, baking bread—and, with a bowl of warmed milk, watch the children's games while you're pressed up against the building walls across from them.

I'm talking about setting off and leaving behind, giving away and receiving nothing in return; to understand me and my demands is to understand that never again will you set foot on Earth and henceforth will have nothing of yourself to return to other than in thought.

Here and now, I'll make it crystal clear that for years the body will turn on its own axis, rotate with vomit on its tongue and, in the hours of its greatest need, will be left like that.

Long will the body yearn for another—pressing a hand between its thighs and guiding its own fluids into the room—and then apologize to itself for consigning itself to eternity, saying: I'm unsure of myself, I'm not thinking as I act again and again. It has to do with the space, with my sudden yearning for my mother and for the mountains that provide shade on July afternoons when the children are running home along the ditch and the cats that claw at the children's skirt hems leap into their mothers' embrace and lap their mothers' dugs clean of milk and water.

The body will ask itself: Where are my mother, my siblings, my home and the coolness I sought when I ran barefoot into the sugarcane fields and, with my face buried in a furrow, did not hear them screaming for me to return?

The body will wonder and yearn and be left uncertain, and the body will have to contend with such silence and such yearning and such uncertainty.

The experiment cleared its throat and said: I wonder, then, is there one such body present at this table?

Afternoon now—the sun swollen and heavy made its way across the fields and along the boardwalk, the soft-drink vendors watched the white tourists with their thick beach towels spread on the sand.

Here and there a laugh, here and there an adult talking to a child and otherwise a steady murmur of languages that the soft-drink vendors had learned to understand but would not think to speak.

Afternoon now and along the beach, the soft-drink vendors looked away and continued working as the white children refused an ice cream and their parents put the ice cream aside half melted; the soft-drink vendors hummed one song and then another while the children poured out the soda in the sand and the mothers wiped their hands, sticky and chubby, with two white tissues that were later left to blow around the beach.

Afternoon now and the large restaurant patios prepared to change into their evening garb, the sun loungers that had been brought out with the morning haze now folded up and dragged all the way back. Just like Milde as a child drew sack and rake across the sand for a few coins a day, the beach cleaners in a thorough sweep would soon gather all the ice-cream wrappers and water bottles—diapers, plastic bags and tubes of sunscreen—and collect every piece of bread and every fruit left to rot but still good enough to be eaten.

After several nights' work, the cleaners would maybe find something to bring home to the Outskirts; maybe something small or nothing at all; maybe they'd find nothing at all for a very long time and then suddenly a wristwatch peeking out of a sand dune or a piece of jewellery glinting between two sun loungers; maybe they'd find the watch and the jewellery and stuff the watch into their underwear and gently place the jewellery under their tongue, allowing themselves to be searched as usual at the end of the night shift, and then walk the boardwalk to the sleeping area, nothing more than a few trees; perhaps the children could then show off their finds to each other and uninterrupted share among themselves what dregs of drinks and bites of bread they had, sleeping a better sleep.

The children from the Outskirts, who at night cleaned the beaches and in the morning went to their trees for a little rest, would in the daylight lie close to each other and cover themselves with their only blanket at hand—sleeping like that the whole day through and waking once more at sunset to start all over again.

Afternoon now and the distant sounds of cars in motion struck the library, the early summer light fading slowly. As she sat facing the window,

Milde could follow the city on its way home and see the square filling with children and adults. Grocery bags, grocery bags and someone stopping for a cigarette break; she saw cats stretched out in the shade, blazers slung over shoulders and schoolchildren crowding at the ice-cream stand soon to be emptied of popsicles. Who'd have thought the day would be this hot, and who knew what the children and mothers of the Outskirts were doing about the heat at this hour? She began to soften.

One astronomer wiped his forehead with his shirt sleeve, drank half a jug of lukewarm water and waited. Another let his hand sweep slowly across the paper, lingering on a sentence, following it.

Maybe the hottest summer in a long time was on its way—the sand had already begun to blow in between the buildings—and maybe the astronomers knew that the following summer they'd embrace each other and lower their voices in anticipation of the launch. They'd watch their screens, loosen the corks and wait for Milde to speak. And when Milde's voice finally broke through between one call and the next, the astronomers with their bottles ready to pop would finally start cheering and cheering more, boasting that the impossible had taken place, cheering louder and even more.

At that point Milde would have embarked on the journey to her black hole the Mass where she, in the darkness surrounding her, would strap herself to a chair or a bunk and from there write more and longer to the Outskirts; she would write to the Outskirts that she loved and that loved her back, and her body in its weightless state would continue to remember the Outskirts' metal floor against her ribs and the Outskirts' mist that in the morning lay like a hand upon her thighs. Her tongue would remember the roughness of the mountain and the fingers that had drawn across Essa's stomach would remember the smooth scars that extended from her belly button; her hand would follow the scars across the paper, strokes that filled it from edge to edge, page after page, and then she'd press the papers to everything in the spacecraft in order to give it all meaning.

Later the newspapers and radio would say that the conditions had been favourable. Around the glossy white table sat twelve astronomers, Milde and a police entity that, in deference to the history about to be made, had chosen not to keep Milde in handcuffs. The room contained no extravagance, no excess of caution, and when the silence was broken it was not by shouting or music coming in from outside—but Milde's hand moving calmly and decisively along the table, drawing the flickering light to her.

Milde said: The image of this moment has long been alive within me—I now hold it close to the whip marks branching like a tree across my chest. What you're describing is not new to me.

For a long time, I've been running hands over my body and bending over my own thighs, kissing them from the inside out so they'll understand that I'm someone else with someone else's voice and hardness in my mouth. My thighs, in turn, have allowed themselves to be deceived—blind to their own ability to rouse desire, they've nurtured a longing for deception and searched for what will draw them into the darkness and then let go.

No, what you're describing is not new to me.

I might wish that what has befallen me would appear like a sheet wrapped around my body—that imprints in the fabric would attest to what the body has lost so far, to what has come to be my face with its hooked nose, domed eye and the hollow left by the other eye, now no more than a shadow in the world. But what is all this wishing for?

Every day I wish to return to my home, every night I want to sleep with my back on a metal floor and Essa's tank top pulled over my head, but what is this wishing for? It's long ago now and since then I've been lonely enough to know that my loneliness exceeds my yearning, and my yearning exceeds my hope for anything other than what I love and know best: my home the Outskirts. Have you ever been there?

Everything except the Outskirts—beautiful as everything and nothing altogether—I am hopeless in the face of. Everything except our ditch—soft as every spring day and every summer day and every grain of oat on the tongue in one—I am now indifferent to.

I know my home as a gulp of cold water and as every mountain at the moment dusk obscures the sun and every sun when at dawn it defies the mountain and rises above its crest.

Have any of you ever been there? Do you even understand what I mean?

As a child in the Outskirts, I wanted to be a teacher, a builder or simply happy. Now that this is all that has become of me, I want to do this correctly and properly—for the sake of my Outskirts.

I want to make the journey, Milde said, setting the candle down on the table and gripping the now-warm peach in her hand.

It could have been any year at all—above the wharf gates the blossoms of the chestnut trees once more flamed like lanterns in the spring, and a haze stole across the shore and lifted a spatter of pink water to the sky.

The city stretched out flat, spent, and like other summers, allowed itself to be swept into a rhythm of breathing other than its own; the surge white and foaming lapped the sandy shore in time with the cruise ships and along the avenues the cafés were once more setting out their tables and opening their umbrellas. Yielding, the beach spread beneath the tourists' white feet as they shuffled between the dense stands laden with soap and whisky. Tired and bored, the standkeepers stood smiling by their carefully stacked goods. This one? I'm practically giving these away, how many would you like?

This was where the mothers and then the children of the Outskirts would usually go: here to the market where, in the shade of the trees lining the boardwalk, they'd spread out a towel and place on it their wares: crocheted washcloths in green and pink, long necklaces made from crushed china and coloured glass, and one or two trivets made from spare books, bottle caps and metal lids. Madame, feel this—the softest cotton and linen, crocheted and dyed by hand. I'm practically giving these away, how many would you like?

At dawn, first the mothers and later the children too would mount the Outskirts' only broken bicycle in order to spend three days and two nights carefully spreading out the towel on the boardwalk on which to display the necklaces and washcloths.

As the third night drew near, the mothers and children under the cover of night would cycle all the way back and once at the foot of the mountain help carry the bicycle up the slope of the Outskirts and in among its homes. There all the other mothers would be waiting with tea and sugar—with bread, butter and coffee if there was any—and with freshly laundered shirts for them to change into.

It was either very late at night or very early in the morning.

It was early enough for the children to be up but far too late for them to want to be asleep, and just as the children continued their play—waiting, watching and running to the slope to see if anyone was walking uphill—the rising sun was like a blue-green blaze over the crest, and so the day began.

Yes, the children and sisters of the Outskirts waited for these homecomers and welcomed them with heated water and mango found among the garbage and cut into small pieces over the fire. Once they'd washed off the city dust and wrapped towels around their bodies, the homecomers were fed the now-warm fruit, which they carefully took in their mouths and rolled under their tongues. They wouldn't have had a bite to eat for a day and a half and hoped, after a good night's sleep, to have a little more to eat here at home, here in the shadow of the mountain that rose black against the red afternoon sky and here beside the ditch that flowed rippling clucking brown and green past the houses of the Outskirts. Here, at home, embraced by their own, with tea steeped over the fire, and next to the walls of the houses, towards which the morning sun worked its way, warming the corrugated metal walls and tarpaulins stretched between the houses.

Later, when the Outskirts had found a second bike to use, the mothers and children who either dragged their coolers fully stocked along the beach or displayed their necklaces along the boardwalk in the evenings would cycle into town together—there would be more of them to do the carrying there and back, more to pick fruit, milk cartons and what sacks of onions there were out of the dumpsters, and more to band together when cars, windows rolled down, suddenly slowed and stopped right across the street.

It could have been any year at all; autumn arrived later than usual, replacing winter, and the water lines were extended and the taps replaced in accordance with Milde's terms and conditions. In the morning the Outskirts waited to hear further news of Milde's impending spaceflight and thus sat down to eat what was there, clustering around Essa's handheld radio on full blast. Had she left yet? Where was she? Would she stop by for a visit first? Who was holding her captive? The mothers and children continued to congregate for months until news of Milde stopped and Essa no longer got up in the morning and no one dared knock on the door, asking to borrow that radio for a while. Then would come the morning when the children who were expecting Essa at school could no longer put up with having an absent teacher and trooped to her door. You have to come back, Mama Essa, it's enough now, the children would say, and on the mattress Essa would lift the tattered rag from her eyes and sit up.

It was the year of the launch and of meals and coffee breaks spent in the canteen of a spaceport, of sleepless nights in the pool and the body that either laid itself down at its own feet in resignation or stretched out on the floor, trying to remember.

Milde ate when she was supposed to and went to bed when she was supposed to—took walks when she was supposed to and showered when she pleased.

The women Milde got to know at the spaceport and who every afternoon invited her for tea and bakes in the staff room—nothing more than a kitchen with five broken chairs and a window cracked open onto the courtyard—kept telling her how admirable she was and how they wished her luck. Milde would look at them and say: I'm doing this for my sisters and for the sake of the Outskirts. So that, if only for once in my life, I may blend into a surrounding that resembles me and live once more in the hope that somewhere out there is a world that wishes me well, a world that wants me as part of it.

Sure, I can go to space and die, why not? I'd rather die in the depths of a black hole than wait around to be executed here, if you see what I mean. I'm doing this so that I can sit back and rest for once, no knife or metal lid hidden under my pillow, and so that, if only for a day, I won't have to look at those same white faces that wish me harm.

Sure, I can go to space and die, why not? I'd rather die there than continue to be of service here, if you see what I mean. I'm doing this for the sake of my sisters and for the Outskirts—for the children and the slope and the cats' yowling as soon as it's bedtime and the mist is pressing against the roofs; I'm doing this for the sake of the washing lines and the washbuckets, and for every tap in every place where taps are rusting away but dammit if they aren't still in working order, do you see what I mean?

The women would put a hand on her shoulder, slide the coffee pot across the table and sit there nodding silently. They would hug her yet again when she got up to leave, and in the evenings they would bring her tea and cake. You shouldn't go to bed hungry, they'd say, and Milde would nod and say thank you.

The nights were longer in the spaceport than in prison, she didn't know why.

This body that for eleven years had been missing its left eye and both index fingers would inspect its broken nose in the mirror and run a hand along its collarbones. It would trace the stub of its index finger over deep scars on its arms, legs and stomach, and in the glow of the bathroom light, slowly count them, as if to then be able to set them aside.

This body would try to remember what the prison pit had smelled like and what the body looked like when, after eleven days, it was finally allowed to wash off the menstrual blood that had run down its thighs and caked like dark cuts along its calves and heels. Milde would try to remember how painful it had been and how pain was measured in those days, according to what measure and why, and how come she no longer measured pain in the same way.

Milde remembered that the places of torture were connected to the buildings where the prisoners lay on a damp prison floor and placed their hands gone cold and stiff under their heads until they went numb and the numbness woke them.

On one such prison floor, across which the prisoners had crawled blindly in search of a corner in which to piss and shit, Milde had also curled up, legs pulled to her stomach, and tried to fall asleep—this she remembered.

The places of torture—where Milde was later woken by her numbing hands and sought out the corner where she'd pissed before so she could piss there again—were just below this prison floor she was now crawling across, scraping her body against in the dark. She crawled to the wetness in the corner, squatted and wiped her hand on the wall for lack of clothing to wipe herself with.

It was in one of the rooms below that prison floor that she'd sat awake on a chair for five days and five nights and repeatedly asked to go to the toilet; she was menstruating.

Milde had said: I need to pee and I'm menstruating, let me go to the toilet.

The blood, a variable flow, had run out of her and dried, she had writhed in the chair and gotten nowhere.

When she'd finally peed herself, the guard uncuffed her, then undressed her and wiped the floor dark from urine and soiled deep red with her shirt and pants frayed at the knees and hems.

The guard then picked up the stained clothes and redressed Milde, lifted her back on the chair and pressed her body now cold in the wet garments against the backrest, hands cuffed behind her.

After that, he'd only approach Milde in order to undress, clean up and dress her. Ever colder and more bruised she'd slide in and out of his grasp, again and again slipping down to the floor and staying there.

When, after no telling how long, the guard

had come over to wipe up what she'd been holding in and had flowed out of her loose and light brown, she'd screamed that she'd rather be naked, they could leave her as she was, Let me freeze to death, don't dress me again, don't dress me again you bastard do you hear me, you make me sick, Milde had screamed and screamed before she was met in the mouth by the butt of a rifle and collapsed.

Later she'd woken to the stench of herself and then to the absence of all sound. That's what it was like to face the pits, and that's how all the sisters with whom she later shared a cell would remember it: They'd opened their eyes in the dark and had found nothing, closed and opened them once again and again found nothing.

In the pits at first each was kept on her own, wounded fingers searching their own faces from mouth to eye socket—pressing their eyeballs to make sure they were there—then letting their hands drop down once more.

The prisoners had uttered something to test their voice and heard nothing. They repeated what they said louder now, still nothing.

They'd stuck their fingers in their mouth and felt their tongue, counted their teeth and wiggled their toes. They'd run their hands along the bridge of their nose, wondering if their nose had always been like this and if so for how long, stroked their hair, wondering if the taste of blood had always been so pungent and if so since when.

The prisoners had lain down to sleep on the damp prison floor and pressed their nose to it, trying to sniff out the source of the damp and whether the wastewater was flowing down the rough walls. They'd wondered if someone else had been in here before them and if so who, and whether they were still bleeding menstrual blood or if the blood was coming from elsewhere.

Milde recalled that only when the cell door had been opened and things were tossed in—first bread, then bottles of water hitting her body—had she realized her eyesight was still somewhat intact.

After that she'd searched for that crack of the door for days on end, crawling up to the door right when it was time for it to be flung open and, aided by the light, had tried to find what gave shape to her gaze and allowed it to navigate.

The prisoners had always shut their eyes at first, thus holding the memory of the crack of the door for longer inside them, bringing it to life between its openings, trying to imagine that somewhere out there was still a sky and a sun, a sandy beach, a sea and cats scampering along the paths cut by mothers and children who fell into each other's arms and did not wish each other harm.

In time they learned to turn away from the door right as the key was shoved into the lock so as to let the light reveal to them something of their cell's interior; the floor and the ceiling, how small they were, the corners and the cracks, what was there.

The prisoners let the light from the crack of the door illuminate the cell and then knew where to go to eat and where to pee—where to stay so the water bottles wouldn't hit their back and chest and where to lie down to sleep when nothing but sleep could help.

Milde recalled that in the places of torture the light would sometimes be tinged blue and sometimes be a dazzling white that stunned her eyes now used to the dark. Later she was unable to conjure up the image of any other light as clearly and on some nights, still blinded, had difficulty sleeping. When one afternoon between coffees she told the women in the spaceport about this shifting light, each one created a memory of her own to bind to it. One said, The morning my mother left me on my own, and the other said, When I was seven years old and got lost in the rooms of the hospital where my grandmother was on her deathbed.

Milde said: The torture room had a marble

floor, grey and white concrete walls, and a steel chair that made the body conduct electricity.

She remembered that her body had been damp the whole time and that she'd fallen to the floor many times. She also remembered the interrogations and her back-bound hands, how the policemen, with cigarettes between their lips, would inhale and blow smoke in the prisoners' faces, stamping the lit cigarettes on the prisoners' nipples then forcing them to scrub their wounds clean with soap and water.

It was said that Milde was the brains behind the uprising, the first to suggest arson and the one who had long been agitating the children and mothers of the Outskirts; she'd been spotted at the scene and was said to be the one who'd procured the rifles and who refused to name her conspirators. This is why they'd stubbed out a cigarette in her eye right before the end of the final interrogation, and she was carried to a cell where twenty new sisters were waiting and was dropped among them unconscious. She was forced to remove the cigarette herself and after twelve days the whole eye with only a pair of nail scissors that someone had managed to smuggle in; afterwards she didn't know what to do with the eye and finally summoned the guard and placed the eye in his palm. The sisters in the cell had clamped her head between their arms, pressed down on her chest as if to make her hold her breath and handed her the nail scissors with care. Milde had in fact held her breath and then collapsed; afterwards her hair was caressed slowly and softly. She stayed with her newfound sisters for eleven years.

In line at the spaceport's canteen, tray in hand, Milde would look at one of the servers and say: Once I ran across the mountain with a rifle over my shoulder and at dinnertime my foot slipped and I fell into a hollow. It wasn't high up, but I was stuck there for hours all the while the sun was lapping at the sugarcane fields and stinging my eyes. Do you know how that feels?

Milde would say: In prison, I found a second home with other sisters and other mothers, and when they called me to solitary confinement, someone else always stood up and said, Here I am, and followed the guard out. And they threw Sabina in solitary and they threw Marisol in solitary and they threw Silvia in solitary again and again. And one day when they called Sabina to solitary confinement, I stood up and said that I was her and gladly followed the guard who didn't notice that my left eye and both index fingers were missing. Do you know how that feels?

It was a year like any other—every day Milde wrote a letter to the Outskirts and lay flat on the grass in the courtyard next to the raspberry bush she'd demanded she be allowed to plant. She tracked the sky with her gaze and kept repeating to herself: Sure, I'm going to space to die, why not.

Milde was led through the white corridors to the room where she'd be housed ahead of the journey and encouraged to make herself at home. She was greeted reverently, directed to various rooms for this and that and anointed daily with salve and coconut oil to temper her skin ahead of the cold in space; Milde was laid to rest for long stretches and slept the whole morning through, was given everything she wished for and wished for anything that came to mind.

She said: I've never had much of an appetite, but I value a hard bed and heavy blankets, black sheets with black embroidery and a refrigerator large enough to hold fourteen bottles of water and some butter. I also wish to have a library, a desk, two gramophone players and four dictaphones with the accompanying cassette tapes. You can also bring me four boxes of chocolate, two bags of frozen raspberries and three packs of cigarettes a day, and don't forget that I appreciate freshly brewed tea and heated milk at all times of day.

All this was carefully carried in by two white professors and cluttered the room early the next morning.

'We apologize, the room is designed for shorter stays, it tends to get crowded.

'Most space travel requires far less preparation, your journey is the first of its kind.

'Call it a maiden voyage, a voyage of discovery—or anything else that comes to mind, it's entirely unique.

'Just don't call it a mistake; that would not be correct.

'No, by no means is it a mistake—be assured that we've spent a long time planning your journey, down to the very last detail.

'The void you will be travelling towards has been the subject of much theoretical analysis, and we can with great certainty say that we know what we're getting into.

'The Mass, as you know, is not a hole in the sense that there is a hollow, something stretching, a furrow that offers shelter.

'Rather, the Mass denotes a gap, a void, an absence.

'As your single eye again and again fails to survey the Mass—where it is and what it looks like—sensations will arrive in your body the closer you come to what seems like something but is in fact a single great nothing.

'Your body will sense this nothing and be drawn to it.

'It will be drawn to it, and nothing you do can ever prevent or weaken its power of attraction.

'No, it's precisely this power of attraction that we want to observe.

'We want to see what it does to you.

'We want to see what it does to your body.

'As such, your journey has no final destination—perhaps it should more correctly be called a ramble, a search?

'It's hard to find the right word, but perhaps it's an ongoing dialogue between us and the black hole the Mass?

'In any case, you'll be drawn to the Mass, and as distant observers, we'll be watching you.

'We'll watch your journey and how at a certain point it will seem to slow.

'To us on Earth, it will appear as though you never quite reach the centre of the Mass.

'Your journey will appear to be endless.

'But this will be an illusion.

'From your vantage point, you'll reach the black hole's event horizon within the finitude, and you'll remember in that moment: This too shall pass.

'Don't be afraid, we'll be communicating with you.

'We'll be present the whole time and keeping a close eye on you.

'However, it's important you understand that at the event horizon you'll no longer be visible to those beyond, and for us, everything but your voice will vanish.

'We'll no longer be able to see your body or follow its movements.

'We won't be able to see your spacecraft or know its exact position.

'Therefore it will be extremely important that you continue to speak—that you continue to describe what's happening and what you're seeing, how it feels in your body and how you perceive the Mass.

'If not, the experiment will be considered a failure.

'Yes, it's very important that you speak and describe what you're experiencing throughout the journey—otherwise the whole endeavour will be meaningless.

'Everything you say will be important.

'Nothing you say will be trivial.

'What we know and what we assume about human bodies falling into black holes is entirely based on theoretical knowledge.

'With your help, we hope to change that.

'Yes, your body is what will provide us with empirical data—now is the time.

'Theoretically, science assumes that a redshift will be apparent in your feet and knees just as you pass the event horizon and travel towards the singularity.

'The science tells us that this should be taken as a sign that your feet and knees are about to burst.

'This will now, in collaboration with you, be either verified or refuted.

'We also assume that an increase in gravity between the soles of your feet and the top of your head will be palpable.

'You won't be able to hold anything in your hands anymore.

'If this is true, your body will change, be reshaped.

'You'll feel pulled apart, stretched out, and finally you will snap.

'In theory, you will burst, and it probably won't take very long.

'Of course, once this happens, there's nothing more any of us can do.

'Precisely when this will happen—where this splitting force is most lethal—we cannot say, unfortunately.

'For a very large hole, such as the one in our vicinity, this point lies deep within the event horizon.

'This means that you might be falling for a long time without coming to harm.

'We want to emphasize that this is our hope.

'While also emphasizing that no matter when the splitting takes place, you will not return here.

'Once you pass the event horizon, there is no force known to us or to the world that would be able to bring you back home.

'Once something has reached the singularity, it exists on a timeline, the end point of which is time itself, and thereafter no other possible timelines can ever lay claim to it.

'No, nothing can retrieve you, and it's important that this be crystal clear to you and that you're clear about this now.

'You will not be coming home.

'You will not be buried.

'Is this clear?'

Milde took sporadic notes, sipped the coffee that had been placed before her by one of the professors and let the other professor wipe up the drops she splashed around her. She kept asking for refills—right away, steaming hot—and every so often stomped on the floor, clapped her hands, shouted requests.

Later, with tidy handwriting, she wrote:

To the children and sisters of the Outskirts

this place is so terribly dull that I sometimes wish

I'd be swallowed up by my big black hole already
and mulched to a pulp

believe me, nothing here is reasonable

believe me when I say that not even the food here
is reasonable

there's nothing reasonable here except the shower
and the bed, the odd cup of coffee and a few
books I've already finished reading

I value a shower and a bed, of course I do, but
believe me when I say that at any time I would
trade it all for a spell of silence and a moment
with you all and our tin cups full of hot tea in
the twilight by the mountain, I want nothing
more than to sit with you by the mountain when
the mountain rises blue and pink, and talk about
what the morning requires while the mist that
has kept the Outskirts in place slowly dissipates
and the starry sky into which I'm headed begins
to twinkle above our roofs

this is my wish, this is what I'd like right now
and in every other moment of my life, and this is
what I imagine at night when I can't sleep

I imagine coming home to you

Do you all see this? Milde had said, pushing out her left eye soft and shiny into her cupped palm extended towards the professors who were now backing away. I need to bring along several similar prostheses. Can you arrange that?

A short time later, Milde was again in the newspapers, glossed up with her hair combed back, gaze steady and shirt neatly buttoned at the collar and cuffs.

She'd summoned the journalists and stood at the entrance to the spaceport's sleeping quarters and had said, voice deep and proud: In exchange for sacrificing my life to the world's most advanced scientific experiment, it seems only fair that I should be able to demand and be granted better conditions for my neighborhood and my people. It says as much in my contract, and contracts, as you know, are binding.

Milde cleared her throat and said: The neighborhood is called the Outskirts and you know where it is. You know the story as it has been presented to you, or the lie of it you've made up yourself. I've already demanded in writing that the water lines be extended and the ownership of the dump be transferred to the mothers and children of the Outskirts—these were the first things that came to mind—but unsurprisingly, I have further suggestions for improvement and therefore want to speak to someone who wishes me and my community well, who cares for the place where my heart is buried and to which I always return in thought, the place perhaps a handful of you have visited at some point when there was nothing else to do and the boss ordered you to confirm a sloppily noted task that you hoped someone else would have taken care of, right? In daylight at some point, you ventured to my Outskirts—in daylight at some point so as not to sully yourselves, right? Don't look at me like that, you're the same clowns now as then but in a different guise—the same disgusting ineffective benevolence and the same shitty tolerance. Don't look at me like that, I've been robbed of so much, it's true, the best years of my life, they say, and it's true: You have robbed me of a happy life in the Outskirts, but you haven't drained me of love or made me homeless. No, no one can drain me of love or take me out of my context and by doing so make me forget the place I belong to and my origins. I do not forget who my mothers and my sisters are and where my soul belongs on Earth—I do not forget where my consciousness was born and how, with bubbling muddy water under my feet, I grew to be this big.

Think of me as your first real contact from the Outskirts, Milde said smiling, Or not. I couldn't care less. Just do as you're told and keep quiet.

She said: Now zoom the camera in on my face—I want to wave to my sisters and send them a greeting.

She said: Friends, mothers, sisters—my only teachers in life as in death—anything and everything is yours, sprung from your bosom towards our shared belief. It is for us that I will be wrapped in the cold and with your help that I will endure, for us that I will uphold my memory and in your company continue to become everything I've wished for myself.

Milde raised her head even higher and said: There is nothing to yearn for here—I'd rather sleep on our floors and eat mashed fruit from your soft hands.

She said: Don't make the mistake of desiring this place, there's nothing desirable here—I'd rather walk up and down our ditch and drink our tea on the slope in winter.

After running a soapy washcloth under her arms and along her thighs—lying on the floor to feel the floor as earth and solidity beneath her—Milde gathered her papers into a pile and poured coffee into a tin mug. She sat at her desk with her back to the window, did not see the desert birds falling and rising in turn and like every other night began to write to her Outskirts.

Milde wrote:

To the children and sisters of the Outskirts

to my comrades, all that I have—
to you whose scent can still be detected on my fingers
(the left hand in particular draws your contours across the table)

to the day that has gone, the day that is to come
my last remaining day   you—

it is to you that I am writing
through your will that I continue to exist

to you who are still packing mud into tins, hurling them across the highway just as the flow of cars into the city increases and the darkness protects you from seeing and being seen—it is to you that I am writing, through your will I continue to exist

I write: Keep doing that
to you who have not yet tried: Start there
to you who have been scared into stopping: Start again

to you who claim that the tin cans are the wrong approach: Don't say that
to you who think it's the wrong approach: Change your mind
to you who first show the children the best way to empty the tin cans and then teach them how best to pack the mud without getting so much as a scratch: You're the ones who have raised me—it is to you that I am writing, by your will that I continue to exist

to you who raised me: You are still raising me
to you who have taught me: Teach me more

to you who know the song we sing as the pigs approach: It is with you that I sing
to you who know the song we sing when the pigs draw near: Teach the children to sing it
to you who know the song we sing when the police pigs draw near: Teach no one else to sing it

to you who remember how we beat and wet the earth: Do you remember more?

to you with marks from metal and wood along your back: How did we keep standing?

to you who lifted me up to knock the metal roofs into place: Do you think I'll forget?

to us who do not forget: What does it matter that everyone else has forgotten?

to us who do not forget: It is to you that I am writing

to us who do not forget: It is through your will that I continue to exist

to you who taught me to remember: Without you nothing would have happened

to you who taught me to remember correctly: You taught me to run with a rifle over my shoulder

to you who taught me to run with a rifle over my shoulder: What we believed is still valid

to you who want to forget: First teach the children to remember correctly

to the children who want to remember correctly: Teach what you remember and then let a friend remember correctly

to the children who remember correctly: It is in you that I put my hope, for your sake I continue to exist to you who teach children not to talk to white men: You are as I remember us

to you who teach children not to talk to well-dressed men: Keep saving their lives

to you who teach children not to talk to well-meaning men: Never stop raising me—it is to you that I am writing, through your will that I continue to exist

it is to you that I am writing—you are the reason why I write at all

it is to you that I am writing—for your sake I continue to exist

to you who teach your mothers to write: Write to me and tell me

to you who teach your mothers to read what I'm writing: It was you we hoped for

to you who still remember my voice: Call me back to the Outskirts—it is to you that I am writing, through your will that I continue to exist

to you who now cry out: My hearing is not what it used to be

to you who wonder why: They stuck needles in my ears

to you who wonder what I did next: I tipped the chair over and made sure to hit my head on the floor—unconscious I no longer felt the pain, and my hands were crushed under my weight

to you who feel unease: Allow yourself to feel unease

to you who still feel unease: You can stop now

to you who no longer feel unease and instead feel determination and a particular tenderness for those like me, who are like us: We come from the same place—it is to you that I am writing, through your will that I continue to exist

to the Outskirts: the dream of once again walking along your ditch and helping our children cross from one side to the other

to the Outskirts: the dream of stepping inside and staying with you

(to me: the dream of once again embracing my mother and for a moment simply being her child)

to the Outskirts that I love and that loves me back

to the Outskirts that I love and that loves
me and itself back

there is still a chance to set
things right

that chance belongs to no one else
    once again it is here in our arms

Later the greengrocer would write that the departure for the black hole the Mass took place on a day that was said to be empty of all else; born to be significant, the day's date went on to grow awesome in size, and unrecognizable to its surroundings, the date took the month by storm and rose to its feet. Year after year it drew the people of the Outskirts to its slope, sitting there, the mothers on blankets and pillows and the children on their feet eager to get closer to the sky, as if standing up would help, as if Milde would then descend and from her black hole reach out a hand to the children and gently caress their cheeks cold with the mist resting upon the Outskirts' mountainside.

The mothers and children turned off the lamps in the Outskirts and, carrying sugared tea in bowls and pots, took their seats on the slope. The lanterns that Milde had demanded the city place there, those they turned off too—as well as every little light in every home and along every bush around the ditch of the Outskirts, leaving the Outskirts in darkness.

The mothers and children then sat on the slope, looking up.

The darkness of night elevated the Outskirts and helped them look for Milde there, in the boundless sky, in that which recalled her and brought her to life again and again. The darkness of night made the mothers and the children forget and remember their bodies, and at once gave them all and no form in the world to call their own.

They were delighted, smiled.

They were delighted and said: Somewhere in the sky is there a deeper darkness than usual?

A spot, a line?

Something drawn along the sky like a scar deeper than other scars or a furrow softer than other furrows?

If so, that's where Milde is.

There she hides from our gazes without deliberately staying away—from there it is possible for her to exist without actually having to exist.

Wave, speak to her.

Wave, smile and remember her—she remembers and misses us back; love, write and speak to her—she exists and loves us back.

It was said that the sky was clear and smoothed-over on the day of the launch and that the surrounding desert had a warm yet bluish sheen, the early summer air both fresh and stifling.

From the launch site nothing that allowed Milde a reminder of life could be seen. No Outskirts with contours for her finger to follow and no corrugated metal floor on which to lie; no prison pits to share and no comrades finding rest in her arms.

There was no weapon and no uprising to live for; no fruits, no sisters, no song. Within reach upon the desk was a thick bundle of her letters and a little farther away three books she'd asked to take up with her. Apart from that, nothing.

She'd gotten to see her mother one last time, that much was true.

In the morning, Essa had suddenly walked in and wrapped her arms around her in the doorway, holding her like that for so long, as if she knew nothing else.

Essa, who'd grown thin and had tied up the hair she kept covered, now greyish silver twine twisted and tamed, had pulled her daughter to her as if from the edge of a precipice and let her hands slide over that daughter-body, squeezing and feeling, pressing her way forward and letting her physical memory determine if it was really true. After what had felt like a thousand years, had she now caught hold of the right person? Did she know these dips and bones, emaciated sinewy arms and hands that had aged ragged and rough?

As for Milde, she immediately recognized her mother, with a child's clarity then as now she immediately recognized her mother and even felt for her hair—let your hair down Essa, let it down for me, Milde had pleaded, and then how that hair, as if of its own accord, loosed itself and framed their embrace.

It was true that she'd been allowed to see her mother one last time and that her mother had wrapped her arms around her more struck by fear than longing, let her cheek caress her daughter's shorn head and brought her daughter to her breast.

Milde said: They advised me to cut off all my hair now, so I wouldn't have to do it when I'm up there, you know. No one will be able to help me with that once I'm up there, you know, no one will be there with me, and no one will be able to help me with anything.

Essa had lain down beside her daughter and let the narrow bunk push them close. She had draped her silvery twine over her daughter's bald head and let Milde stroke it as if it were her own. Essa said: Feel—this is what your hair would feel like if only you could grow as old as me. Can you feel it? This is how your cheek and your neck and your arms would feel, this is how your stomach would feel if you had a child as beautiful as mine.

It was during one of these moments that the door was opened and the water brought in, that the towels and the soap were brought in, the sheets and the book.

They were placed at one end of the room and Essa gently led her daughter there and undressed her. She then undressed herself, and once naked, she soaked the washcloth in soap and water and walked it over to the emaciated daughter-body and placed it in Milde's hand.

Essa said: I've always imagined you gently washing my body when I am dead. I imagine that your movements would be very smooth and thorough and you would take your time. You'd talk to me and I'd try to hold your hand—you'd caress my arms and breasts and in that moment know that this mother who is on Earth is ever-present everywhere that is not Earth.

Essa said: A daughter should wash her mother after her death—that's how it should be. There should be no complications and nothing should disrupt this order. You and I now face a complication, my love, and so now, for want of later, we will do what is right and proper.

The day after the launch, the mothers who worked in the sugarcane fields got up at dawn and walked down the slope; those who had cycled into the city during the night were already halfway there, and Essa, who in a few hours would open the doors of the school shed and welcome the children in, leaned against the mountainside with a large glass of tea and the photo of Milde in the newspaper pressed to her chest. Essa had asked the Outskirts to carry on as usual, saying that Milde would have wanted nothing more than to see the Outskirts going about life as usual and this was now their duty. The mothers had nodded and hugged Essa, asked to see the photo of Milde yet again and left Essa to sit there.

With her shirt neatly buttoned at the collar and her shorn head hidden under a scarf, Milde in the photo was standing outside the spaceport's sleeping quarters, looking past the cluster of cameras and microphones. Essa sought her gaze, angled the newspaper as if to better catch it, and then pressed the photo to her chest again. It was the most beautiful picture of Milde she'd ever seen, as beautiful as the one of her sitting in her grandmother's arms on her second birthday, looking straight into the camera, and just as innocent and clear.

The children, who'd gone to sleep by the entrance to the gas station so they could ask—the moment it opened—if they could take all of yesterday's newspapers with the front-page image of Milde, had just run all the way up to the Outskirts and placed the stacks at Essa's feet, then sat quietly beside her. The children, who'd been sleeping outside the gas station, had at night watched the stars and the black hole the Mass, wondering how far Milde had gotten in her spacecraft and whether they'd ever find out if she'd arrived.

Many years before, Milde had graced the front page of the newspapers, her hair as cropped as now but younger and with both eyes intact; she'd been photographed at the time of her arrest and during the trial and then in the moment the verdict was delivered, and everyone in the city had cheered at every bad word uttered about her. All the photos had been awful, of course, all taken as if the camera had been hurled at her young face and in the corner of each picture white policemen and at the bottom a glimpse of Milde's hands bound behind her back.

Essa looked at the now-yellowed newspaper clippings. Her daughter's eyes did not shirk from anything, looking above and beyond every camera flash and, as always, with her head held high. How had this been possible? How had such boldness come out of her own body? Essa lay down on the metal floor, the place where she and Milde had played, eaten and argued, slept deeply.

The children who'd been waiting at Essa's feet finally asked for a newspaper to take with them. Then they had their breakfast on the slope to better demonstrate how far in the sky Milde had come and why she was that far at the moment and not farther than she was. How do you know she's got that far, one asked curiously. What if she was going at super speed and has gotten twice as far? Someone shook their head and replied: She was launched yesterday, right? So that got her all the way over here, and in the night she managed to get all the way over there. She must have been going at medium speed, not super speed, because the body can't handle super speed.

Yes, that sounds right, one replied, while another lay down in the dust and said: I don't think so. I think Milde's body *can* handle super speed. I think right now she's all the way over at that end of the sky there, all the way over there above the mountain but deep in the sky, so far away that from here it almost looks like she's touching the mountaintop with her spacecraft even though that's impossible.

Yes, the children—who every morning thereafter ate their breakfast on the slope so they could follow Milde's journey and feed the cats who as always this time of year had grown tired of soured milk in large bowls along the edge of the Outskirts' ditch—could see one morning that yet another highway was being built, this time right through the sugarcane fields and past the border to the caves where Milde had once been in hiding.

Then the children jumped up, ran.

They pretended to remember the uprising and reconstructed it, interrupting themselves and saying: My mama said it was like this, jumping up and saying: My mama said it was like this, like this and like this, see? See what I'm doing with my hands? Yes, just like that—that's exactly how it went, and this is how they got away.

The children didn't argue or get sad mid-play, they just played more and longer. The children didn't cry and didn't want to switch roles in the middle of the game, they just added more scenes and then began again.

The children spoke and reconstructed and then ran to the school shed in the Outskirts where Essa was already standing in the doorway to welcome them in. Today the school day would be about Milde and the uprising, and the children who'd heard the story many times before wanted to hear it again.

Outside, the mist settled over the Outskirts.

Behind the bushes that adorned the banks of the ditch—at the lower branches that either bore sour gooseberries or nothing at all—sawed-off rifles were still hidden.

Under the metal floors of the houses—where Milde had once been a child and, like the other children, had been woken up by the cats' soft tongues on the soles of her feet—the root cellars were still full of gunpowder and gasoline.

MILDE IS SEVENTEEN YEARS old and sitting cross-legged in the middle of the cave. Until now she has always turned towards the desert, searching for something in the desert that reminds her of the Outskirts—a shift of blue like how the Outskirts used to shift between pink and blue, a misty heat like how the mist used to heat the roofs and walls of the Outskirts—but now she no longer wants to see the desert or have anything to do with it. She's tired. A month has passed; she knows all about the desert and nothing here reminds her of the Outskirts. Not its dryness, not its expanse, not its solitude. Not the way the screams never become screams and the food never becomes food and sleep never becomes what sleep is when she's close to Essa. She's tired. Instead, she sits facing the cave and from there tries to conjure up another time, another place. She can tell by the light in the cave what time of day it is, and she never has to turn back to the desert, no need to face the desert, never again must she turn to face the desert unless she wants to, never again for as long as she is there. She no longer knows if time matters or if time is all she relates to. She lies down, falls asleep.

Now and again—as she waits for one of the mothers or children of the Outskirts to cross the cane fields under cover of darkness and pay her a visit—something moves in the corner of her eye that reminds her of a rat or a cat in the bushes of the Outskirts.

She wishes for any of them to come and closes her eyes to conjure them; give me a rat or a cat, it doesn't matter which, and then let me open my eyes in this place. Give me both of them without them fighting and then let me hold them close as a mother or sister would. Give me back my mother or Diamond and Trinidad and then let them sit beside me as I draw my days on the cave floor. Let them take the drawing back with them to the Outskirts and describe it to the children who I love and who love me back. Let the children remember me where I sit now, almost invisible, existing for nothing but memory. And then let memory not fail me for as long as I live.

MILDE, THE GIRL FROM THE OUTSKIRTS

What is a home? The Outskirts is my home, Milde would say.

Enveloped and shrouded in the mist that descended and beaded morning dew in the hair of the people who lived there—on the mountain where the mountain suddenly plateaued, opening up to its own scattered greenery—the Outskirts existed as a buzz to dampen the city sounds.

With its metal sheds, it was something both new and old to the world; it looked out at the world and then turning around, closed in on itself, becoming something soft and warming; and then, kept blossoming, facing the world but only in part.

Have you ever been there?

Adorned with tattered scraps of cloth to shield from the sun between the rooftops—and lined with shrubs from the ditch down to the slope and back—the Outskirts rose from the garbage with its green and purple homes, wrapping itself like an embrace around the mothers and children who, in the morning and evening, thanked themselves and each other for having built the Outskirts and turning it into home.

For each pillow a sharpened knife and for each slipper a slingshot to aim at tourists in their cars who stop at the foot of the mountain, looking up with curiosity.

The Outskirts, where the scent of bird cherry mingles with that of scorched earth and garbage.

Have you ever been there?

What is a home? The Outskirts is my home, Milde would say.

It was here, at the edge of the map, but not exposed.

Here—next to the border and the city's largest garbage dump, from where brown water was sent running through the doorways and into the ditch—was the Outskirts, nestled in a soft groove between mountain and desert, and casting a warm light upon itself.

The Outskirts rose up from the earth as small sheds made of sheet metal and wood that spliced and sealed the gaps in every wall already sealed many times over, and their wide-open doors welcomed the children running home.

As beautiful as itself and nothing else, the Outskirts in the autumn received the mothers, squatting to wash their homes of dirt and sand and making sure the grass tall around the houses continued to keep out the rain and mud.

The Outskirts helped the cats into the shadows in July and wrapped itself in winter like a warm embrace around the mothers and children; it trod a path through the tall sugarcane field where the children could always hide, and dug furrows for Milde to sink into when she fled her home shortly after the uprising and could hear the police dogs' ever more distant barking.

Have you ever been there?

Milde is eight years old, the Outskirts is a newborn in her arms. She goes up the slope, steep and almost endless, and looks out. Farthest off are mountains, before the mountains is desert, and before the desert is the sugarcane field sharp and dense. She pauses. No, that's not right. Farthest off is the border. Then come the mountains, after that the desert, and here, closest, the sugarcane field dark and billowing. It's her birthday and she hasn't been able to sleep. She has never celebrated her birthday here before and doesn't know how to do it. Last year it was just her and Essa, just like the year before that. Now she will be hugged by the mothers and children, and she doesn't really know what to do or say. On the bedside table in the old house was a photo of her in her grandmother's arms, the birthday cake with flaming candles and in the corner of the frame an accidental glimpse of Essa's finger. This was before her grandmother died and long before they came here. She doesn't remember much about it and today she doesn't care to remember either. It is dawn in May and soon Essa will follow the ditch to the slope and find her there. Milde will get a diary for her birthday—she already knows this because it's the only thing she has wished for and never has Essa been unable to fulfil her one true wish.

Later, with a week to go before the uprising, when Milde was about to turn seventeen and for the first time hadn't wished for anything for her birthday, Essa, who'd spent days preparing the clothing and maps Milde was to take into the city, would remind her child that a birthday was a birthday and not to be neglected because an uprising was underway. Essa wasn't speaking plainly—there might not be another birthday to celebrate—and instead suggested she cook a proper dinner with what the Outskirts had saved for the winter, dried eggplant and okra, sliced mushrooms and powdered milk. Milde would shake her head and lie down on the mattress in the middle of the room, saying that she had been wishing for the uprising for years and that nothing could compare to having that wish fulfilled now and forever.

The Outskirts, where the houses are hidden behind the mountains and the afternoon light colours the place red and pink—have you ever been there?

What is a home? The Outskirts is my home, Milde would say.

How big the Outskirts was and how far it stretched was impossible to say.

The earth where the dead were buried was gritty and did not accommodate deep graves, and on the banks of the ditch that ran along the Outskirts, vegetation rose from the thick wastewater, making the greenery exuberant and heavy.

The cats, carefully bred by the Outskirts, roused in the cool afternoons each with a rat in its mouth, while the rats brought in with the garbage moved like shadows through the dump just as the mothers of the Outskirts got up and began to go about their day.

It happened one morning that Trinidad's mother did not wake up and Trinidad ran through the homes, gathering the Outskirts around her.

This happened, and later that day Trinidad fell to the ground and would not move for a long time, would not rise from the earth muddy after the night's rain and would not be carried into the homes by the mothers who sat beside her pleading.

The days when the mothers did not get up in the morning to the sound of Essa's ladle hitting the bottom of the pot almost always ended with the children also being given evening tea with sugar and fresh mint. The children rolled mango under their tongues if there was mango, or bread and butter if there was any to spare; they spent the night in the arms of other mothers and were not left alone during the day, were taken to the sugarcane fields if they wanted to sneak a lick of sweetness and were carried up the slope once they'd grown bored of this and wanted to go back home.

The Outskirts washed their dead mothers with a stump of store-bought soap and water heated over the same fire where the tea was simmering, then wrapped them in the sheet the mothers themselves had washed and hidden away, and carried them gently to the burial ground at the foot of the mountain.

They looked at the maternal body, soft and gnarled, and ran their hands along it—then pressed kisses to the arms, legs and into each palm, and let their mouths linger between her breasts.

Sweet tea keeps bad thoughts away, the mothers said, pouring it the moment the burial was done.

Tea is nourishing and keeps you warm, comforts and softens the joints of those who've shovelled and dug, shovelled and dug, and who for days afterwards can't help but look at the fresh grave from time to time, wondering whether it's even and properly packed, whether it's deep enough for the dead to rest in, and whether the head is in fact resting in the direction where heaven can come lay its claim.

We will always wonder if the graves are deep enough to prevent us from going there at night and, under the cover of darkness, digging our way to the ones we miss so that, with blood under our nails, we can lie down next to them and sleep together one last time and never again—just one last time I want to sleep next to her and then I promise never again.

Here, drink, Essa said, handing the glass of tea to Trinidad, who silently accepted it and wiped her face with her shirt sleeve, setting aside the shovel and sitting down to rest beside it.

What is a home? The Outskirts is my home, Milde would say.

At the base of the mountain, it was along the ditch made deeper by the children's playing feet—close to the metal walls that slicked damp against the cats' yellow fur, brushed and wet—that the cats of the Outskirts slowly moved, taking short steps between the mountain and the berry bushes, sharply defined in the dawn light and seeming to mark the beginning and end of the Outskirts, and then leapt over the garbage as the garbage trucks dumped their loads and the rats hiding between each bag and box bounded forth, revealing themselves.

Under the children's sweaters, worn from play and sunlight, the feline bodies climbed slowly over their tummies and up to their necks, pushing their heads through the rings of their collars torn at the edges, to rest their chins on the children's shoulders.

Shortly after the school day's end, just as the sun weighed on the quilt of tattered tarpaulins patched with scraps of cloth so they'd stretch from one home to the next, the children walked along the ditch, calling out to wake the cats and beckon them.

In the tarpaulin shade, casting shreds of sunlight through where the fabric was worn or torn—upon cardboard boxes large enough for them to sit on and with each door ajar—the mothers of the Outskirts gathered to keep each other company and, in the cool shade, to do what the day required of them.

The one who was responsible for meals in the Outskirts today sat with two bowls in her arms, sifting bugs and grit from the flour. The one who'd just taken the laundry out of the tub and let the water run cloudy and foaming into the ditch would soon be hanging the lines with sheets, towels and underwear, and the one responsible for mending socks, tops and shirts was leaning against a wall and letting a shred of light fall upon her hands. The stitches that attached the cloth patch to the shoulder strap and gave it colour would later gleam on the wearer's shoulder in the sun as she washed the dishes with sand or took off the top to rinse out the sweat in the water running down the mountainside, hanging the top afterwards to dry.

The mothers of the Outskirts had the pile of clothes and the sewing box to hand, reaching for a sip of water from time to time and cutting off all the loose threads with a pair of dull scissors someone had managed to take on a day when the scrap dealer was looking the other way and no other customers were standing by. The oil is not fresh, but it'll do the trick, the scrap dealer had said—I siphoned it the other night from a car parked on the boardwalk, and now you can have it at a special price. And the mothers had haggled and paid and taken the can under their arms (scissors pocketed) and went on their way. The mothers had walked up the slope towards the Outskirts where the electric generator was beating away and said There are indeed parked cars along the boardwalk at night, shall we go there on Friday and do a little siphoning? The other mothers had nodded, and the mothers with oil cans under their arms had gone over to the generator and tended to its needs.

It was in the tarpaulin shade that rolled out between the homes in the morning and rolled back when the sun turned lukewarm that the Outskirts worked in a hum and then put down the fruits of its labour.

As the children stepped out into the dense cane fields, hands shielding their faces, to collect and carry home the leaves the farmers had raked into piles, the mothers of the Outskirts would walk down the slope and wait for the children to return. Later, one of the mothers would drag the car hood out from the back of a shed and place it upside down across the ditch, almost bowl-shaped, filling it with the leaves from the sugarcane fields and letting the leaves catch fire.

Still in the afternoon, one of the mothers put aside one mended tank top and picked up another to reinforce, while another took the pile of clothing under her arm and sorted it correctly.

Whoever was in charge of the meal finally put down the sifted flour and unfolded newspaper as a work surface, picked out potatoes, carrots and apples from all that the Outskirts had carried with it from the city and took out the knife small and sharp from her back pocket.

Those who'd been scavenging garbage the whole morning through wiped their faces, necks and arms, weak from carrying their loads, and the children who'd carried armfuls of leaves through the cane fields ran off to play. The mothers who'd just returned from the dump laughed and talked about what they'd found and what that city actually bought, can you imagine, can you imagine that's what they buy, the mothers said and laughed, and the other mothers shook their heads and laughed along.

The mothers who'd wandered across the dump unbuttoned their shirts and sank their feet in the cool runoff water in the ditch, drank a cup of tea. The mothers who'd sat down to cook kept cooking, and the mothers who'd patched the Outskirts' clothing stood up and ran a damp cloth over the back of their neck.

In the afternoons, just as the children came home and left their schoolbooks by the pile for all to read and share, the cats, awaiting the children in the shade next to the working mothers, would wake from their slumber and emerge.

The cats would make their way to the children's feet and let themselves be stroked and squeezed, and the children would lie down in the soon-to-be-yellowed grass and feel the weight of the long feline body on their chest with sighs that slowly put them both to sleep.

Later, after the police began to patrol the slope of the Outskirts and in the darkness force their way into homes where the mothers who'd heard them coming were clutching their children in their arms, the cats would disappear over time, leaving the dump unattended. The children who saw the policemen grabbing the Outskirts' cats by the scruff of the neck and putting them into sacks and carrying them away would run after them, crying, pulling at the yowling sacks, kicking the policemen's legs before they were pushed to the ground.

The mothers who wandered the dump in the Outskirts could no longer let the children come with them on their search; the rats that had proliferated and bit the mothers' heels and calves could easily bite off the children's toes, and the children who no longer had the cats to play with often knew no better than to bend down from time to time and softly stroke the rats' fur.

One day Sofia's daughter was bitten and came down with a fever that none of the mothers of the Outskirts could quell. The Outskirts collected money in a purse and carried the child down the slope along the highway and among the whitewashed houses that marked the beginning and end of the city. They walked with the child moaning, being passed from arm to arm, until a truck pulled over and agreed to give them a ride to the hospital in the centre of town. On occasion the hospital asked for papers and then the mothers and children of the Outskirts would tell them that they had no papers—None of the kind you'd consider valid anyway, Essa said, lifting the child over the counter, but her name is Nina and she needs help, and my name is Essa and I can pay.

What is a home? The Outskirts is my home, Milde would say.

Around the Outskirts was a mist that expanded along the entrance not as a gate but as a promise, and a sun large and veiled that lingered above the mountain and let the mist rise and enfold the Outskirts.

The roofs of the Outskirts always were the roofs of sheds under the mist and the bushes dewy even in the afternoons. Clothing in the Outskirts never did dry fully and hair was forever standing on end, but skin between scars shone as if oiled and feet stayed smooth.

It was said: Such is the mist over the Outskirts, and so it came to be, so soft it is, and so spread out across the mountains and bushes of the Outskirts.

It was said: Shapeless and soft moves the sky that protects a place beset with mist, and smooth and heavy rests the Outskirts in dazzling fragments that hold everything in place.

Have you ever been there?

Every roof in the Outskirts was high enough to keep residents upright but no higher, low enough for them to repair the roof where the roof needed repairing after autumn and winter rain and no lower.

Every corrugated metal floor in the Outskirts was laid slant so the water would trickle out the door and into the ditch, and every little camp stove was set on a stool next to some platters, their edges cracked, and plastic cups stacked high.

There were green and pink bowls, there was an empty honey jar and a steel measuring cup to drink from if you wanted to. In the summer in July, in the summer just as the sun hot and large finally sank over the Outskirts and the water running down the mountainside was the only substance that was still cool and clean, the measuring cup then collected the water and kept it cold for the Outskirts, filled itself back up yet again and continued to keep the water cold for the Outskirts.

The promise was softness, shelter and coolness.

Have you ever been there?

It happened that the children, who had wanted to help the mothers repair the walls and ceilings where the moisture had seeped in, were beaten by the men at the gas station whenever they'd been lucky enough to find scrap metal to carry on their backs all the way home.

This would fix a hole or two, the children thought, and hurried through the back streets towards the fields and the steppe, but they only got as far as the gas station before they were beaten to the ground and what little they'd found was taken from them. The children then walked up the slope crying and threw themselves into their mother's arms, resting on a bed of blankets and pillows and spending a long time reading the book they'd been lent. The children went out of their homes and into their Outskirts only when the evening mist had thickened, and the dusk that gathered the mothers for tea along the ditch began to fall, drawing the children out to the foot of the mountain to play. The children played, stopped to talk about the scraps they hadn't been allowed to keep, and then played even more.

Milde is eight years old. She wakes up on the metal floor where the mattress is wet from the mist that has run down the metal walls and throws off her blanket. She then gathers her hair into a bun and rolls up the sleeves of the shirt she has almost outgrown, checks the bruise from yesterday's beating by the gas station owner and then puts on socks. Later that night, for the first time, she will go into town with the older children to spend two days and three nights dragging sack and rake across the beach in hopes of finding something to take home to the Outskirts. She will do this, and on the way home she'll hold Trinidad's waist tight, sit happily but tired on the cargo rack and watch Trinidad's feet pedal through the darkness.

Before leaving her home, Milde shakes the ants off her slippers and writes three long lines in the diary Essa gave her. Outside, the mothers work on nailing together new homes, and on the slope, children play with a ball. Everyone greets Milde as she walks along the ditch to the tap with her cup, and at the farthest house is Essa, waving at her. It is May, and from the slope you can see that the trees by the roadside are in bloom.

Later, when the Outskirts could no longer draw water from the only tap around, the mothers who worked in the sugarcane fields would ask the sugarcane farmers to share. Yes, only a little, they'd say—just a drop until we've fixed the tap—and the sugarcane farmers who were watering their farms right then would fill three canisters and one or two bottles for the mothers to take with them. That's all I have, the sugarcane farmers would say, and the mothers would lift the canisters onto their backs and go their way.

Later, when Milde was fifteen years old, she would gather Trinidad and Diamond around her in the evenings to plan in earnest the uprising they'd discussed as they cycled to and from the city. In the first instance, Milde was to set about talking to every aid organisation she could find and ask them all for money.

No, we don't need any discarded clothes and shoes right now, but we could really use money for shelter, food and water. Do you have that?

Milde would converse with them at length and occasionally let one of them come along to the Outskirts' slope to have a look around. When the time finally came—when she was finally going to get the money in her hand—they'd first offer Milde a sum and later ask her to pick up the money in monthly installments. Sure, absolutely, why not, Milde would say, putting the money in her pocket.

First, she'd have the tap repaired, then divide up the money between the mothers and finally put her, Trinidad and Diamond's share in a box hidden in the root cellar under the metal floor at Essa's.

When the time came, she would take out the box and, together with Essa, ask the sugarcane farmer at the far end for some rifles, just for hunting hares and large desert birds, Essa would say, and the sugarcane farmer would bring four rifles so they could start practising.

What is a home? The Outskirts is my home, Milde would say.

The children and adults of the Outskirts would wake up in the morning and gather each other's hair into buns, approach the bowl placed by the wall and, aided by the wall, collect the night's misting rain as water to wash their faces with, and carry the bowl inside.

They woke up and as if possessed sang little songs of the beauty and joy of the Outskirts, and then dressed themselves in the finest garb available; removed a patterned shirt from a nail driven into the metal wall damp and cold and picked out the only pair of pants torn at the pocket and along the hem where it had been dragged up the mountain.

At the same time as the morning that brought with it water with which to splash the body fresh and cold, song arrived in the Outskirts—with the sound of bowls being taken out and filled with one part milk and four parts water and with chews of coconut bread mixed with nuts plucked from the beach hotels' dumpsters and carried all the way home.

The mothers of the Outskirts let the children eat their fill and then gathered their schoolbooks into a pile; they made sure that their pencils were sharpened, their sweaters tucked in, and that the socks they'd mended the day before were pulled up over the scabs, cracked and red at the ankle.

Later, after the end of the school day, the children would cycle all the way into town, stuff their backpacks full of fruit, rice and bread, and eventually make their way home.

In the shadows along the avenues, where a cat or two was stretching out in the warm grass and the dogs were on guard at a distance, the children would wait for the darkness to fall at any moment—still only the beginning of the summer season long and insufferable—and watch the streetlamps light up across the city.

The children would collect straight twigs for days and then repeatedly throw them into a pile to play pick-up sticks in the grass. When it was time to leave, they'd carefully tuck the sticks into a thin plastic bag tied to their waistband and run the back streets to the hotel dumpsters wide open and full for them to climb into.

The children of the Outskirts learned on which days the hotel's old bread was thrown away and the fresh fruit was replaced in the bowls in the lobby, when the hotel restaurant served pork noisette in large pans for lunch and raw chicken was tipped out of boxes straight into the dumpster and rendered unusable for no reason at all.

The children who slipped around on the chicken in search of something anything to take home or to eat in the moment got better with each night at knowing where that something was.

Something anything left in its packaging even if the package had been torn open, or in its bag even if the bag was broken and something was moulding; they were looking for something half ripe or half rotten that they could cut with the jackknife the oldest children had on them just in case, or something lukewarm and tart with which they could quench their thirst, if only for a moment. Perhaps a yellow mango or a cucumber hard somewhere in the middle and otherwise soft; maybe a packet of melted ice cream to share or chili sausage to shred and boil in a big soup with salt and sugar at home in the Outskirts.

When they were on their way home, cycling the last bit in the heat with no water in their bottles, the gas stations would shoo them away more angrily than the outdoor cafés, and the sugar-cane farmers with houses along the road would not open their doors at all.

The children found their way in anyway, crawling through the dense shrubbery, shirts pulled over their faces, to the well with its wooden lid, scoop and pump in the middle of the garden. They managed to pump the bottles half full before someone walked out and threw a slipper in their direction, shouting that the police had been called and next time there'd be a rifle to answer to. The children then hurried away and left the garden the same way they'd come in, pants muddied at the knee ragged and thin, and their arms covered with more scratches from the twiggy bushes and thorns.

Diamond would lift her sibling back onto the bike and calmly pedal on. You did well, she'd say, and share what little water there was between the two bikes that now continued out of the city, the sun at their backs and the broken backpacks full of what they'd managed to carry off.

Later, the hotels smashed glass bottles against the walls of the dumpsters and let the shards fall among the boxes and food, thinking this would scare the children away.

The children who in the evenings helped each other up and over into the dumpster would at first not notice anything at all and then feel the sole of their foot slit open from toe to heel with the piece of glass still inside. It happened sometimes that a passerby might call the ambulance and then the police, looking around for help and calling out to others who had also stopped. It happened, and the woman who'd called the ambulance would wrap her shawl and then her cardigan around the foot of the child of the Outskirts who'd been cut this time. She'd tell them to contact their parents, You do have parents who can come get you, right? The children of the Outskirts would see the police approaching and form a circle around their sibling, shielding her from the eyes of the police and saying, Yes, we do; we have mothers, and they'll be here any second.

It happened later that Milde opened her eyes on the grove where they'd curled up at night, each waiting to drag their own cooler across the beach, and saw a shadow fall from behind her back and upon Trinidad's sleeping body. She shut her eyes again, not knowing what to do, and carefully reached for the knife she and the other children kept between their thighs and pulled out when they didn't know what else to do.

Milde knew that the pedestrians on the boardwalk below wouldn't help even if she called out, and that the morning that had brought with it the light and the white men on their way to or from the beach wouldn't lay cover on the smallness of tired girls. She knew that the sun that had risen above the treetops would not then retreat as a favour to them and that the cover of night they longed for would not sweep in so they would at once be concealed again.

It's happening, Milde thought, wanting nothing more than to have Essa beside her; it's happening, she thought, gripping the knife.

Later it happened that the grove where they'd always gone was no longer theirs and the men and boys appeared at all hours. The men and boys slept on the children's flat sleeping spot and sat on the children's worn tree stumps and grass, did not pick up their pants when the children screamed and spat, and only half turned away when the children threw stones bigger than their palms at their bodies.

It happened, and the children, watching as the men and boys grew in numbers, asked their mothers for help. The mothers who next trip followed the children to the grove first threw tins of mud and then took out knives, stabbing at the now doubled-over bodies and did not stop until the men and boys backed away and disappeared. The police who accompanied the men and boys up to the grove repeatedly took the mothers in and the children who didn't want to be left behind clung to their mothers' skirts and cried. Dragged along a bit, they were then taken in their mothers' arms, and after that they left the grove for good.

Milde is nine years old and has just cut off her long hair. It's morning and she opens the metal door in front of her and steps out, looks around for the other children and waves, I'll be there soon, wait.

She goes to the ditch and sees Essa with the shovel a little farther on, greets all the other mothers, who, like Essa, are digging the ditch deeper and rounder every day, and throws herself around her mother's neck, I've slept well.

She hurries to the slope to play for a while before breakfast and when she returns, Essa has just washed the dirt off her arms and legs. Milde takes out coconut bread and a piece of cucumber, puts the kettle on the camp stove and fills it with tea leaves and water. Later they walk together to the school shed, Milde a few steps ahead with her writing pad in her arms and Essa with the day's textbooks in broken rattan baskets on her arm. Later, Milde and Trinidad will head to the beach to work and be away from the Outskirts for two nights and three days, but right now—right as the new sun is making the place drip with dew—she runs up to the school shed, throws open the door and hurries inside.

What is a home? The Outskirts is my home, Milde would say.

It was in the morning with the mist that the song arrived in the Outskirts—first there was the buzz of conversation about the day that was about to begin and all that it would bring, then buzz became song, and song arrived in the Outskirts.

Those who were going to the beach to do business made sure that everything was in place and that the broken strap of the sun visor had been repaired. The person at home who was to crochet washcloths for the Sunday market by the sea made sure the yarn would stretch beyond its capacity, and Essa, who was to gather the children in the school shed, struck the bottom of the pot with her ladle on her rounds through the Outskirts, drawing the oversleeping children along with her.

The children sat on the cool sheet metal in the classroom in the summer and on plastic mats the whole winter through; they would pick up their writing boards and pencils and watch Essa write a question on the cracked slate.

It happened that the children who'd cycled all the way home from the city didn't have it in them to go up to school some mornings and instead waited for the sound of their classmates walking along the ditch on their way home. They'd open the door and pull one of them by the sleeve, say come, tell me, what did you do today?

The children knew that nothing escaped Essa, but they still had no desire to go to school with a forearm swollen from a baton blow or a foot slit by glass in a dumpster. Instead, they stumbled between bed and the teapot and lay down on the mattress with their bandaged foot, reading themselves to sleep and not waking until dusk had descended on the Outskirts and the mothers who'd been waiting for them to come out stroked their cheek and told them to get up. Time to eat, come.

Milde is nine years old. It is spring, February night frost and March bushy green. The school shed has just been constructed, and the tent that was previously used as a school has been torn up and made into tarpaulins to hang between the roofs.

Milde sits on the sheet-metal floor with the other children listening to her mother. In here my name is Essa, Essa had told her, and Milde wants to remember that. She shuts her eyes and silently repeats it to herself a few times, then opens her eyes and concentrates. Essa has written something on the slate and all the other children are trying to copy it down. Milde knows this word and writes it four times in a row before putting down her pencil and waiting for the next one. She knows that in here her mother's name is Essa and that Essa is also called Miss and that Miss sometimes asks her to read aloud from the book she has chosen and that then she'll stand up, solemnly holding her book. Milde reads a paragraph and then asks should I keep going, Mama?, she can't help it. She has to stop this, she knows it, and that's why she practises saying

Essa or Miss, Essa or Miss, Essa or Miss several times and does not stop until she thinks she has finally forgotten how to say Mama.

What is a home? The Outskirts is my home, Milde would say.

In winter, the mud of the Outskirts reflected the sky, and the sky darkened to a brown that only the mist could soften and spring could ease. Slowly the birds circled the sky, attracted by the dump, higher with each passing day, and softly sailed towards the children and mothers as they worked or played.

The children let their hands be hammered by their beaks and claws, and pulled their shirts over their head as they hurried away, running fast back and forth across the Outskirts and finally following the ditch's dark waters home.

Barefoot on narrow paths—past the garbage piles in the mud that stained their pants hems the colour of the sky, over rock and raspberry bush ready for pruning, past clothes hung to dry and in among the houses—the children hurried.

Doors made of reinforced cardboard and canvas were shut and the children in the homes were counted; if the mothers brought in an extra child or if one had accidentally run too far, they'd pull the canvas aside again and call out: Sofia is here with me!

The mothers took out an extra bowl of coconut milk and cut up yet another tomato from the tomatoes found in yesterday's garbage that had not had a chance yet to moulder or freeze; later, the mothers ran a cloth over this child's face as well as their own and dried them with the same towel, combing the child with the same yellow comb; the mothers oiled the child's lips, cracked from the cold, with the same silky oil and swapped the child's wet socks for socks in the same size as their own.

It happened that the children grabbed each other by the sleeve and said, Come here, let me show you something, and the children went behind the canvas—where the laundry tub stood and the toothbrush and the soap stump—and saw the other children pull up their shirt to reveal a wide wound swollen over a tummy both soft and hard. The children asked, What the hell is that? and the children replied, I got it when I was searching the scrapyard the day before yesterday, found an engine but it was too big and when I tried to get it out I hit my tummy like this. The children showed each other and the children asked why don't we go there and try to get it out together?

Milde is ten years old. Throughout the Outskirts, mothers continue to build homes, storage rooms and kitchens out of wood, sheet metal and plastic that they've carried in turns all the way home from the scrapyard.

It happens that the mothers get a lift from a truck driver to the slope at the Outskirts and the truck driver helps them up; sometimes the scrapyard behind the gas station has something useful and the aid organisations that Essa speaks with when she is in town lend her a car to transport the city's scraps. Sometimes the aid organisations buy planks, nails and tools for them to work with, and this specifically makes Essa happy. Essa says: For once they're listening to someone like me after so many years of dismissing us. Forever dismissing us, all the times we went to them to warn them of what did finally happen—They're talking about deportation, we told them, do you understand what that means? They're talking about taking us across the border and leaving us there, they're saying we have to go home, but what home do we have other than this one, I told them. I was born here and my child was born here, I told them—it's true that we've been living without papers for all these years, but now we're being deported—is that acceptable? These are our lives, I told them, but no one wanted to listen and so we ended up here. Milde listens to her mother and sits down beside her, watching the buildings rise one by one, wishing she already knew how to build a home.

What is a home? The Outskirts is my home, Milde would say.

In the mornings in the Outskirts, Essa would say to her daughter: Come, darling, let me rinse your eyes.

She'd gather Milde's hair into a bun and orient herself in her daughter's face at once still the same and in constant transformation—younger and older with every twitch, at once familiar and unfamiliar. Essa would trace with her fingers the swell of scratches from bushes and carefully, with repetitive movements, run the wet cloth over her daughter's mouth, neck and cheeks, kissing her again and again on the forehead.

When Milde was older, Essa would just as carefully dab at her daughter's face, bruised by the beach guards or by passing tourists on the boardwalk where Milde slept away the sunshine hours in anticipation of evening and the work that would then begin; she would wash the dried blood from Milde's hands and feet when she had cut herself on the glass shards the hotels had strewn in their dumpsters, or had been kicked when she and the children of the Outskirts would sit under the trees in the afternoons, eating their supper of bread and apples and waiting, once again, to drag the cooler across the beach.

In the morning, the mothers of the Outskirts would wake up with their daughters next to them and say: Come, dear heart, don't be afraid—I've told you about menstruation, and now it's here. Shall we wash ourselves together or would you rather be alone?

The mothers and daughters would take out the sheet that the mothers had hidden away long ago, high up enough for moths not to settle in, carefully spread the sheet over the metal floor, flaking here and burnished there. They spread the sheet out so it covered the space from corner to corner, then they'd take care as they folded it in half, once, twice.

Hold it up, let me see, the mothers would say and then, Yes, this will do.

The day their daughters started menstruating, the mothers would gently smooth a sheet out, like a holy shroud, over the floor of their home.

They would tear the sheet into long strips and put the strips in a pile, cut a plastic bag into two large pieces with the only scissors to hand and give these pieces to their daughters.

The mothers of the Outskirts would then say: Wrap the plastic around the gusset and then the piece of cloth, and the daughters undressed from the waist down and fixed everything in place.

Milde is ten years old. Essa runs the rag over her neck and cheeks and asks her to read aloud from the book they've borrowed. Milde is eager and reads well, struggling only with long sentences and the occasional word she doesn't understand. If she'd been hit in the mouth, she'd slur her words, saliva dribbling from the corner of her lips where a red wound was still healing, and she'd wipe away the liquid with the back of her hand. Milde lets Essa braid her hair in two thick braids and changes into the large hand-me-down tank top. At night, she steps out of the tank top and moves closer to Essa. When she wakes up, she loosens the braids no longer stiff against her neck and gently smooths the top with her hand, sets it aside.

Milde, Diamond and Trinidad would plan the time of the uprising according to their menstrual cycles and set a date when none of them would be bleeding.

They'd feel each other's bellies, sleep together for weeks and wake up in time for their afternoon tea on the slope where all the mothers congregated.

The children, knowing that the three of them would soon be leaving but not yet understanding why or for how long, clung to the girls' feet and tugged at their shirts, asking them to come here or there and telling them to read this or that. The children would say: Read it again, Didi, again but this time louder and slower—and Diamond would pick up the book she'd just put down and begin again.

The children of the Outskirts prepared for the uprising by staying awake the whole night through and never accidentally talking about the uprising in terms of the uprising it was. They learned to turn the day on its head and understood that once the day had been turned upside down, it would one day be turned back, and everything would be normal again. A day when they'd no longer have to keep an eye out for white men or police cars along the slope and when the Outskirts—by turns now anxious and excited—would go back to being itself but even more so and even better. Soon, thought the children as they went to bed at dawn, soon everything will go back to being normal, to being better.

In the days before the uprising, Milde, Diamond and Trinidad would let the mothers in the Outskirts feed them white rice and store-bought butter and agree to run laps along the ditch to build up their endurance. They would let their thick hair fall in tufts past their mothers' hands and spend a long time in front of the Outskirts' mirror shards trying to get an idea of themselves in the clothes they'd need to wear to blend in with the city. Cropped short and neatly combed, their hair would be no bother when the fire one night spread through three of the five floors of the city planning office and after that the entire Ministry of Education and one or two of the embassy buildings next door.

Milde is seventeen years old. Diamond is sixteen years old. Trinidad is twenty years old.

Diamond crouches in the bushes opposite the city planning office and casts an eye in every direction. She follows a pattern of turning her head to the left (waiting), straight ahead (waiting), to the right (waiting). She keeps doing this constantly again and again, not knowing if this will all take forever or be over in a flash; she turns around, repeats the action, and then again as many times as necessary before the smoke rises and rolls in.

It's either very late at night or very early in the morning.

Everywhere is dawning but it is still dark. There's a noisy chirping of birds, but nothing can be discerned in the dark. She wonders who is awake at 04:13 on a Tuesday and then thinks about herself, Milde and Trinidad and what they're in the process of doing. She thinks of the mothers and children of the Outskirts who are now drinking their tea on the slope, and of the children who've known for days that something was coming but were not told what. She thinks of all this, keeps looking around and soon sees narrow green streaks filling the sky, below them a stretch of smoke like a pillar rising above.

Diamond stops, notes that the city planning office is now on fire, and then turns her head to the right.

MILDE IS SEVENTEEN YEARS old, and the cave is cramped. It's stuffy now and Milde jolts from sleep whenever it starts to settle in. More than once, she finds herself on the verge of throwing herself off the cliffs, setting herself free. The afternoon sun still the same and the day still day; how long has she been sleeping and where is she heading? The cave still the same cave and the clothes still the same clothes—the desert still the same desert and the longing for the Outskirts still greater than she could ever have imagined. She has lost all sense of her body. She stretches, makes herself as tall as she can to find out if she has grown any in these past months, but soon realizes that she knows nothing about her body when she's alone. She knows nothing about her body's appearance or behaviour in the absence of Trinidad and Diamond and being able to press up against their bodies, and knows nothing about how a body moves and yearns if those movements and yearnings can't be shared with them. She does not know what she's like without Essa and the mothers to return home to and hug, and knows nothing about herself without the children to take in her arms and carry home up the slope. She cannot say how tall she is without pointing to a space between one bush and another along the ditch where she used to rest in the afternoons, nor can she say anything about her arms, legs and hips without looking at Trinidad then Diamond and Essa, and finally at herself. Milde is exhausted and more than once is about to throw herself off the cliff in order to, in falling, feel something fresh against her face—some air, some coolness against her face—and stands for a long time at the mouth of the cave, assessing. How long has she been here, how long has she been sleeping, and why is day still day?

Milde has not seen her own face for almost two months and doesn't know if it's recognizable. She has stopped going out on the steppe to slowly seek out a sand dune or a bush to rest by, and she has stopped pressing her hands against the dryness of the bush and then against her face where everything is burning up. She has stopped embracing the bush like a child to be carried, spoken to and cared for, and has stopped seeking out scorpions, snakes and spiders to track with her gaze and try to pick up. Night is all she longs for, and to be able at night to sit at the mouth of the cave and gaze at the starry sky, learn to love it, dream of the coolness between one celestial body and another in the starry sky, and the darkness between one light and another in the starry sky, and learn to know it.

The next time Essa visits, Milde is all packed and ready to go. I'm ready to go, Mama, Milde says, standing up, I'm ready to come home now. But Milde isn't allowed to come along this time either. Not yet Milde, Essa says, not while they're on the slope keeping watch with their cars and patrol vans, with their rifles and riot gear and everything else they want to use against you the moment you appear. Not yet, but soon, Essa would say, wrapping her arms around her child, thinner and paler with each visit, her hair big and matted.

A few weeks later, when Milde decides to come home in spite of it all, she makes it halfway up the slope of the Outskirts before floodlights turn night into day and everything stops. With a weapon in her face, she fights for air, handcuffed, face pushed into the dust, she is picked up and thrown into the patrol van, which drives siren blaring away from the slope and the dump and away from the Outskirts, which for a moment she thinks she can glimpse.

MILDE, THE GIRL FROM THE CITY

WHAT IS A HOME? The Outskirts became Milde's home.

It was here one day that the mothers had been driven in trucks—here by the border one day before the Outskirts had even begun to take shape as an idea and all the mothers and children knew was that the city was no longer theirs to return to.

It was to here—a border—and there was no Outskirts to boast of yet.

Was it in the autumn with the first night of frost?

Had the chestnuts already fallen to the ground and did the air smell of the sea again after yet another stifling summer?

Was it in the winter, just as the snow that occasionally overwhelmed the city settled over deserted fountains and park benches along the city's avenues? Was it cold in the trunk of the car they'd been forced into, and had they huddled in each other's arms to keep warm?

Could Milde later remember which book she'd chosen to read from that day and if she happened to forget it in her school desk at the end of the school day? Could she later imagine Miss going through the school desk when it was clear that Milde would not be returning, and could she even remember Miss's different facial expressions, Miss's lips, Miss's hand?

It was one day in May, at first like any other day in May; the mothers and children who'd later build the Outskirts were driven to the place on the mountain that would thereafter house them and told to wait there.

In the city's schoolyards, the same flag flew over the same swings and the same soccer field, and everywhere the same sun and the same clear blue sky stood high on that day in May. Everywhere the same jasmine shrubs rose up along the streets, festooning the city with scent, and everywhere the same tourist buses went around the city centre on this Tuesday, on this Tuesday in May at around two in the afternoon with the same light and the same shouts across the courtyard, the same leaps and bounds and the same soccer ball and the same bicycle that Milde had long wanted but never had a chance to wish for as a birthday gift, only seven years old, her legs tired on this day in May, only in first grade and thinner than most as she walked home down the pavement, thinking.

Like the other children left on the patch of earth that would later become their Outskirts, Milde hadn't had time to change out of her navy-blue school uniform when, shortly after the end of the school day, she'd walked up the hill and into the apartment building run down and darkened by dust.

Milde had walked up to the building, its paint flaking, splendid creepers growing down the balcony parapets, and spotted her mother standing in the doorway with two white soldiers on either side and the women of the neighborhood around her.

She'd rushed over to Essa, who immediately took her in her arms, caressed her cheek and carried her inside.

In the corridor of the building they shared with three other families, Essa had then said: They've come to get us, and I'll help you pack. Come.

Milde is seven years old and lets Essa lead her up the stairs and into their room at the end of the corridor. It is the month of May. Her armpits are sweaty and her mouth is drier than usual. Essa sets her down on the floor and she stands in the middle of the room unsure of what to do. She can see that Essa has already packed everything. She has packed everything of her own and everything that is Milde's, the bag is already filled with Milde's things from the shelf and the wardrobe. Essa has not left anything of Milde's in the room and Milde has nothing to arrange. She doesn't know what to do and therefore feels like having a big, long cry. Essa kneels down and takes her by the shoulders, looks her straight in the eye and asks Milde to look at her. Essa tells her what's about to happen and why, while stroking Milde's cheeks. She tells Milde what Milde can and absolutely cannot do, and Milde listens and tries to remember and learn as best she can. She isn't allowed to leave Essa's side until they're in the truck, and she isn't allowed to talk to the soldiers who are taking them away. She is allowed to be scared and horrified even as she is trying not to be scared and horrified the whole time. She must not go off with anyone unless Essa tells her to and must not be afraid of being alone for a while. Be sad, Essa says, embracing Milde, and cry if you want to—crying is nice and wonderful. Essa says: Come into my arms whenever you want and cry as much as you wish—crying is nice, freeing and harmless. Essa picks her up from the floor and kisses her on the lips.

Milde nods.

Milde is seven years old and looks around the room that has been her home, lets Essa carry her out and all the way down the stairs.

Ten years later, in the corridor of the apartment building they once shared with three other families, Milde stood with one bag in her hand and another across her back, now tall and striking, now seventeen years old and her head higher than most and well-dressed, hair short and very tall and very striking.

She stood outside that great entryway and knocked on the door.

Milde asked for the only person Essa had mentioned, and someone let her in and let her walk down the hall to the same living room and see the curtains hanging there, different curtains than before; yes, the hall was the same hall, the curtains different curtains than before, but the stairs leading up were the same.

Milde would remember this: The banister—still ornate but now stained grey and broken—first rose ten steps and turned, then three more steps and stopped. She remembered that it opened onto a corridor long, narrow with a red-striped carpet leading to her and Essa's door, and that shortly before the deportation she'd sat on the windowsill, which she'd increasingly used as a desk, and drawn a large heart with her and Essa's initials in capital letters inside. This is Essa and Milde's room, the drawing was meant to communicate, and she'd pull out a chair and hang the drawing on the door with a piece of tape.

Milde remembered that the last door, next to the closet where she'd often hidden herself in play and in earnest, had been theirs. Perhaps the doorknob was still the same, perhaps the window facing the courtyard was still hard to open. Perhaps there were still guest mattresses in the closet stacked high for her to climb up on and there cover herself with a sheet so as to be hidden from view the times someone flung open the door, searching. The times someone other than Essa—who would first give her signature double knock and then carefully call her name—was searching for someone in the closet and in the bedroom, on the roof, in the basement and in the storage loft right above the stairs. Essa's friends had hidden there many times, Milde remembered, but not towards the end, no, not at all towards the end—then almost no one came at all and when Milde hid she did it for fun and when someone came searching it was Essa in play or in earnest.

How often had her legs dangled from the banister while she was waiting for dinner or hiding from the guests who'd first taken off their coats at the foot of the banister and then gone into the dining room, illuminated and decorated for the evening. There she had sat and played with paper or glass marbles and jumped up as soon as the doorbell rang. She'd rush into their room and lock herself in just as Essa said she should when Essa was not home and then listen to the voices below—were they familiar or new and was it possible for her to come out as usual at some point during the evening? Eventually, she'd lie on her tummy on the bed and, with her papers in hand, keep drawing and writing, begin humming a song and keep trying to write it down, begin thinking of a house and trying to draw it.

Now she was standing at the same banister and waiting, looking around.

The woman who came down the stairs was unfamiliar, they embraced, looked each other over.

Could this really be Milde? The same little girl with her hair styled in carnation-like puffs and a gash on her left knee that needed stitches right away?

Yes, it was.

God bless, the rumours in this neighbor-hood! So many years, so long ago since you'd seen each other. It was said that all deportees had either been killed or banned from entering the country, and since then no one had turned up. Where are you two staying, how are you both? Essa is so often missed here, so often has she been mentioned—what joy to know that she's alive, what happiness to have you here!

Milde slowly filled up on the sponge cake the woman had set out and told her between bites that she was just passing through on her way to the annual market in the mountains, and the goods in her bags would be sold the day after tomorrow, but it being so far she couldn't get any farther than here before dark. Essa had advised that she could find a place to sleep here, any bed, it didn't matter—just somewhere to sleep for the night if possible and then nothing more. Could she possibly do that? Was there space for her to sleep here, Milde asked and was embraced.

It was the night before the uprising, and in her bags, Milde had a pair of shoes and six litres of gas, she had three sawed-off shotguns that could shoot and one other weapon that no one had yet dared put to the test. In her bags were also empty bottles, which she filled with water early the next day, and two changes of clothing for herself—one set all black and the other the neatest the Outskirts could procure (a light blue polo shirt and cotton shorts, Essa's shiny gold chain, and a pair of pale cloth shoes two sizes too small). She'd wear them as she, Trinidad and Diamond moved through the city centre the next day, and when it got dark, she'd change into the black set and move under cover of night towards the city planning office high and large.

What is a home? The Outskirts became Milde's home.

This was how the deportees were once cast into green tents on the mountain, sharing blankets and mattresses but each with a pillow.

The place that would later become the Outskirts was initially scorched earth and fine gravel that had laid itself over the grooves of the mountain, as if the mountain wanted to break open a space where the broken could rest and live; there the deportees were dragged from trucks and left on the mountain one day in May.

It was both cool and sunny hot.

There was no dusk and no evening to rouse the scent of the flowering mountain shrubbery; the sun sank in place and made night against the dawn, which let the wind die down and turned blue the hills, now shining and smooth.

Across the sugarcane fields that already then stretched between this place and the desert, sounds other than city sounds were heard, and when winter later fell from one night to the next, the mist would settle upon the tents and linger, embracing them.

When spring came, and summer, and autumn, and another winter, those in the tents would realize that the mist would never again leave them and they'd join together and become one with the mist, begin to live with and within the mist, and from the mist fashion a sky and in this mist build themselves a home.

On the tent floor where they'd been thrown and knocked swollen, the deportees woke throughout the night and initially sought not another body but another gaze in which to recognize themselves.

They sat up and said, I don't know where I am, can you tell me where I am and how to get back? Then they got up to the sound of cold like a rattle in their bones and joints, and writhed doubled-over the whole night through. The deportees soon realized that the now-cold earth beneath them was alive—that it hardened and chafed the more they struggled and beat themselves at night—and that it allowed their bodies to go numb and flatten in pace with their growing sense of loss and desire to return.

Essa would not be among those who beat herself at night, no, not because of this, not because of a deportation, no, no way; as long as the city existed and the sky existed and the air existed, anything could still happen; as long as she and Milde ate, slept and woke up together, the road to the city could once again open up and reveal itself to all those who now neither knew the way out nor the way in and whose crying was heard through the tents at night, more stained and worn with each passing day.

But Essa hadn't left anyone behind in the city either, had she? She had no one there whom she missed and longed for, and no one who wished she'd come back.

To hell with all the white party members and to hell with the neighbour in the next room and to hell with everyone who claimed to be against the deportations but never spoke up again. To hell with the reporters who occasionally wrote a column and shirked at any other time and to hell with the foreign press and their so-called pressure. To hell also with every aid organisation that she'd applied to without getting help and to hell with those who'd invited her to speak about her situation right before what they wanted her to talk about took place. Trash all of them, she'd think and embrace the weeping mothers, brew tea for them in the coolness of the tent and talk to them about what the city had actually done and how it had repeatedly denied them so much of what they needed to exist and function. Do you remember, Essa would ask, taking a big sip of the hot tea—do you remember how it could have been and how it never was, in spite of everything? Don't forget now just because forgetting suits us for the moment—don't forget just because forgetting is possible right now.

Essa had settled in very soon after being pushed out of the truck upon arrival, the truck which, like a hunted animal, had ploughed along the roads ever more sandy and blinding the farther they got from the city, not longing to return to what she'd been forced to leave. Later, Essa would say that she'd sensed the deportation as Milde would come to sense the black hole the Mass: with her body. Essa had neither cried nor allowed herself to be carried into the truck but had simply wrenched herself from the soldier's grip, lifted Milde inside and then climbed in herself, extending her hand to the neighbourhood mothers who were tearing at the soldier's clothes and said: I'll see you again.

The children—who had never before ridden in a truck and never before been this close to the border they'd heard so much about—tumbled onto the truck floor at the slightest jerk and got up, tumbled and got up and tumbled twice more before they were finally fished up by someone anyone and wrapped in a tight embrace where neither crying nor whimpering made any difference. There they then sat for the rest of the journey and were not released to the floor until the vehicle had come to a complete stop and the door opened up to air and sunlight.

Outside was a wall of mountains with greenery high and rough against the ankles and already yellowed in spring; there was a barely beaten path with rocky hillocks on either side and a patch of sand and gravel where several tents had been pitched.

Essa lifted Milde off the truck's floor and smoothed away the hair from the child's forehead, scraped red and swollen after her tumble. She took Milde's hand and let herself be pushed up the mountain by the soldier behind her. Once they got to where they were going, she lifted their bag from the dust and sat on it warm and soft, letting the child approach all the other children who were also wearing their school uniforms and looking around curiously.

Milde approached the place and looked at those who, like she and her mother, had also sat on the bags now squashed and warm—emptied of almost everything but the essentials—and then hurried back to Essa. Soon all the adults gathered in one group and the children in another; soon all the adults went over to the soldiers and asked for something to drink, saying, We are thirsty and want water, saying, Give us water now, and planted themselves in a circle around the soldiers.

Milde is seven years old. The place to which they have come is almost no place at all, and she has never encountered anything like it before. Well, maybe she'd seen something similar once on TV—maybe once on the news in a discussion about people fleeing and Essa had explained to Milde about where and why. She looks around and goes quiet inside. Essa is standing nearby, talking to a man with a gun. Milde wants to run up to her and say that this place reminds her of the one on the news but doesn't yet dare. Not so long as he has that big gun slung over his shoulder. Instead, her eyes fall on a child her age standing across from her. The child is wearing a uniform from a different school and shoes with tattered edges. They look at each other. Then the child turns around and runs to a group close by. Milde sees that they have a red ball. The children run with the ball, sometimes screaming—jumping up, rushing forward and sometimes falling down. They get up quickly and play even more and longer, kicking the ball between them and running after it even more and longer. Milde moves towards the group and stands on the edge, still looking on. She wants to tell them that she wants to join in but doesn't quite dare yet.

What is a home? The Outskirts became Milde's home.

This was the way the deportees were tossed—out to a place unmarked on the map and therefore hard to refer to.

By a soldier, younger than Essa's youngest party member, Essa had been referred to a tent but refused to have anything to do with it, no, impossible, not here. Essa had pulled the large shawl from her shoulders and wrapped it around her neck and along her short-cut hair soft yet rough; she'd rolled up her sleeves, unbuttoned her shirt stained and damp at the collar and asked to be allowed to wash, immediately.

The soldier with his hair cropped short at the sides and a sweaty collar had finally shown her to a tap gnarling out of the ground, and she had knelt down and let cold spurts run over her head and neck—over her nose, eyes and chin, and down between her breasts, unbuttoning then re-buttoning her shirt.

She'd soaked her shawl and only half squeezed the water out—gently pressing it to her head and underarms—then hurried back, calling all the other mothers to her and saying there is water here, come wash, urging them to come before the soldier started pushing them away, saying there is drinking water and a tap for washing, come, hurry, wash!

Essa had then stood by the tap and turned it on and off, patiently keeping the young soldier at bay as others arrived to wash off the day's dust and wash the children's clothes, now damp and cool on the skin, and helped to wash the children, enlivened by the cold water dribbling from the corners of their mouths and over their stomachs swollen and firm from hunger.

Shortly thereafter, Essa had asked to be shown around, Tell me where you've brought me and what can be found here, show me what is beyond this place and tell me and my daughter what we're meant to be doing here.

She'd called Milde over and washed her child thoroughly, afterwards letting her dry in the sun with other children, and once again stood before the soldier. Come on, show us around now—I presume it's the least you can do. What is this, for instance, and what's that? Who sleeps here and where do the tents come from and where will the children go to school? Where do we wash and where do we get food and where do we go to the toilet? We do have a toilet, don't we? Where is the phone booth and where do we take our complaints and how long are you going to keep us here? You'll be letting us go soon, right?

Essa had circled the area twice, half listening to the boy who mostly just answered 'here,' 'there' and 'I don't know,' and finally planted herself by a tent across from the first one.

She'd said: This'll do, I like this tent. It feels sturdy and proper; I've got a gut feeling about it. It seems to have lived a life before me and is dark enough and big enough and close enough to the gate without being right at the very front. Moreover, it seems to me that the tent is calling my name, saying: 'Essa, Essa—pick me! Pick me Essa, just do it!' Can you hear it too?

Essa smiled broadly and said: It is my right, you see. Picking out my tent is my right, and in this moment, I have nothing but these so-called rights at my disposal. So I shall dispose of them, in time, and be very happy to do so.

A camp stove, a pot and a kettle of stainless steel. A large bowl, four pairs of cutlery and a wide mattress for them to share. Milde and Essa had been given two blankets and two pillows, a pair of sheets each and two tin plates. Essa had also brought two dull knives and an ice box and asked for the weekly delivery of water and gas rations—'Other foodstuffs are in the tent at the guard post and orders for all other needs are to be referred to the next delivery, understood?

'Now try to live frugally and don't waste water and salt—your rations will last long enough so long as you don't put on airs and live moderately. Plan your meals carefully and don't spend too much time in the sun. There's no school here, all this shouldn't take very long. You'll be moved across the border as soon as we've reached an agreement and over there you'll be able to do what you like, it's all the same to us. Once you've been taken across the border, you'll belong entirely to them, and what you do there is of no concern to us. Understood?'

Essa closed the tent and very soon settled into her newfound home. As if she'd been convinced that this was where she'd end up, she settled in; as if she wanted to go nowhere else, she looked around and familiarized herself with her new home.

Essa stretched out on the thin mattress of her chosen tent, placed a hand on Milde's forehead, warm and damp, fell asleep.

Later, the Outskirts would learn that the mountain itself was largely what made the city seem more distant than it was. With its back erect, the mountain both shielded the Outskirts from the city and the city from seeing the Outskirts—in its own shadow vast and dark the mountain made it clear to the children that whatever lay beyond the steppe and the field was none of their concern. Well, it was true, Milde thought in retrospect, but wasn't the city still there, within reach, a day's bike ride away; it was there as the two of them later walked down the slope with their bundles and saw the end of the mountain and the start of the road gritty and rocky; it was there as they later fastened the bundles to their bodies and mounted that broken bicycle someone had stolen and which always carried them in and out of the city in spite of everything, Trinidad on the saddle with the bundle fastened like a sack across her chest and Milde sitting on the cargo rack with hers in her arms, keeping an eye out at the back. Here comes a truck, careful. Here comes another one, watch out.

Later, after the highway was built, followed by the roadside cafés and little by little the whitewashed houses with courtyards, the blue swimming pools—or a sense of a blue swimming pool—would catch the eye of the Outskirts from even very far away, the bike ride into the city would become both smoother and more difficult to endure. After this and all too often the honking cars zipped by faster than ever, all too often they were recognized by the café owners who refused to serve them tea or water even though they'd put their money on the table—how Milde later regretted each such visit and felt stupid, later, when the uprising took place, and she hoped never to be recognized by anyone ever again, later, when she and Diamond and Trinidad made their way home after the uprising and didn't want to be recognized by anyone at all on the long way back; on foot this time, on foot through back streets during the day and when the streets and the day ended with great strides far out into the farmland and steppe that took over when the city and the whitewashed houses petered out; there, on foot, in tall grass that brushed her face as they dark-clad snuck through the fields and took the road behind the closed gas stations with only a few steps between them.

Milde is seventeen years old. Diamond is sixteen years old. Trinidad is twenty years old.

Trinidad knows that sitting in the bushes behind her is Diamond, keeping an eye out in every direction—she knows that Diamond is following the movements that they've been practising for months and so never needs to check to see what Diamond is doing or where Diamond is. As for her, she's standing next to Milde with her bags wide open, half filling glass bottles with gas. She hurriedly fills one bottle, registers Milde stuffing its neck with a rag and then reaches for another. The gas flows onto the grass and disappears, Trinidad opens another canister and does what she has to do at a furious pace, no time to count, and when the canister is empty, there are probably twenty filled bottles lined up in front of her. No more, that's enough, she says to Milde and puts the canister down, we don't need any more—this is enough.

They look at each other and know it's time.

The sky is streaked with green but dawn has yet to come, the birds are chirping loudly from the leaves but no one else is awake yet.

What is a home? The Outskirts became Milde's home.

In the dust-green tents—where those who would later build the Outskirts slept their first night, until enough nights passed for them to start calling the tents 'home' and the mountain a shelter—a darkness descended that was so dark it was as if the Milky Way had disappeared from the sky that was made up of the tops of their tents as well as the world, hidden beyond the space that had become their space in the world.

Almost as if there was a lack of space, the tents had been pitched and the path had been trodden; in the mist without hard walls or floors, the deportees lived in whispers that wanted to hide what should not be spoken of and keep at bay the fear, the worry and the loneliness; on the mountain where the mountain had flattened itself out for their sake, the mothers and children fell into each other's arms the moment the lamp was blown out, staying like that through the night even if they'd rather not have.

In the wind that pummelled the mountain, its strength multiplying a thousandfold as wakefulness took root in the earth that would later become that of the Outskirts, the wind guard loosed itself and soon settled in tattered folds over the body of the tent. The sound of thick fabric against fabric woke those who'd just dozed off, and soon the mothers lay awake in the tent's murk with nothing to see but images of a city, a sea and streets lined with sun-yellow streetlamps that made the jasmine erupt with fragrance and the boardwalk shimmer.

Eventually during the night—when they'd run their hands along their children's bellies and found their breathing to be calm and steady—the mothers would throw off the thin blanket and scramble out of their tent, gasping for air. They'd make their way to the slope that began and ended in darkness and look out at what was as yet nothing but would shortly thereafter be a major highway construction. They'd stretch out their arms and watch them flow into and become one with nothing, lie on their backs on the earth and gaze at the stars now finally visible between mountains and clouds and clouds and moon and catch as many as possible in their hands.

When the mist that accompanied the dawn began one day to thicken and settle over the place silent and dark, the mothers rose from the dust and found their way back along the tent rows, sleeping through the morning and into the afternoon as the sun hot and dry played atop the children's heads and scorched their hair. The further into the summer that the summer slid and the farther away the sea sent its cool breeze, the longer the mothers slept and the more the children played in the sun.

Thank God for the mist, the mothers and children would come to think, Thank God for the mountain that offers us its shade and shelter.

As time passed, the cast-out bodies reached for one another, warming each other's backs and bellies, saying now it's your turn to hold me and mine to be very still—falling into a softer sleep.

Alone and not far apart and with their ribs against the thin mattress on the cold ground, the children also lay awake or slept a dreamless sleep uninterrupted. After the fourth night, when they undressed and stood under the water of the small tap, where they washed their armpits and their chest, the bruises from the cold appeared like cuts along each rib, apparent in their thin young skin, each of the swellings large and thick.

In the morning, the children stood next to each other and lifted their sweater, gently tracing their fingers along each mark, from one side of their belly to the other, where the blue suddenly stopped—footprints like prayer beads in the dust as they circled and inspected each other's bodies—and gave precise descriptions of the bruising.

They inspected each other and said: This is where your mark ends—right here is where your one bruise stops and here's where another starts.

They said: What does mine look like, can you check? They said: I'll pull up my sweater so you can take a good look.

It would hurt each time their mothers carried them in their arms, asking if they wanted to stretch their arms out and play airplane, they would always answer yes and laugh, pushing away the pain until it finally passed and suddenly one day they got used to it. It passed on the day when the cold retreated, hiding now as small fever blisters under their young skin, their young bodies thinner with each passing day; then—when the cold found other ways in and caused inflammations and perpetual colds to instead be what the children knew best—any pain would only be felt in the wounds under the skin that reddened sometimes and sometimes turned blue, that swelled, softened and hardened sometimes, and that constantly made themselves known as an itch deep inside them.

At the same time the mothers who had until this point been mostly concerned with caring for and clothing their children would begin to marvel at their own changed voices and from where the roughness came and why, marvelling at their own rasping and coughing and from where the thick mucus came and why.

The mothers marvelled at their slowness, put their hand over the children's chest or stomach—is this the source of the pain? The children paused every now and then to swallow several times, pausing again and coughing a few times; the mothers swallowed and coughed and had a sore throat and chest every time they sat down with each other and, with a cup of tea in their hands, talked about the days—about sorrow and loneliness, about time, suffering, desire and loss.

The mothers made sure to turn the children over at least three times each night as if to trick the cold and make sure it didn't gain purchase on the children's bodies too much or for too long, bodies cold and feverish at the same time. They woke up and tucked the children in anew, turned them on their backs when they'd been sleeping on their sides for too long, and then on the other side when they'd slept on their backs for too long; the mothers woke up, turned and fell back asleep, and this was how no one side ever became more painful than another, and no child sicker than another.

And sure enough, the children would wake up and feel the stiffness in their legs a little, but eventually not at all; suddenly none of the pain was left, and they were happy and laughed and got ready for the day—a friend was waiting outside so they could go off and spend time together, and Milde dressed as quickly as she could and pushed her hair out of her face, stepped into the dust that hit her eyes and mouth each morning and then headed to the slope with the other children.

For a long time this worked very well—Essa knew the motherly trick, which she shared with the other mothers during the day and could hear being carried out through the tents in the evening, after the lamp was blown out and the whole row of tents lay in darkness.

At night the child should be turned and in the day dressed not particularly warm but just right—the child's legs need to get used to the mountain wind and the ground sharp and cold, and the child's feet needed to feel the roughness of the gravel to be tempered and so endure.

Yes, that's how it is, Essa said quietly to herself and set Milde on the mattress, giving her a kiss. After that she wrapped a towel around the child's belly and back and lay down next to her, pulled the covers over them both and fell into a light sleep. During the night she woke up and turned Milde over, fell back asleep, woke up and turned Milde over again, fell back asleep.

Only on one night did she forget herself, a night of fatigue and gloom, when she dared slide a hand between her thighs and hold it there, almost inaudibly under the double blanket, the movement of the hand that even in the grave-like darkness should not cast a shadow on the walls of the tent, the child who could wake up at any moment and herself, her thoughts and feelings, what were they and where did they come from, this desire and longing, what did they look like and where had they been hiding?

She'd been quick and then lay awake, trying to hear if anyone might have been standing outside or happened to pass by, if anyone had seen or heard her, and if Milde hadn't been sleeping after all and now was confused or didn't dare ask.

The next morning she woke from the best sleep she'd had in a long time to find Milde pale and curled up in one corner of the tent, she immediately pulled the child back to the mattress and laid her body over her. Essa pressed the child cold against her own warm belly and massaged the child's hands, arms and legs; she held, stroked and squeezed, and with kisses sucked the blood back into circulation throughout the child's body hard yet limp.

Only when she heard Milde whimper did she let go, look at the child then run outside.

There was still nothing with which to spell 'The Outskirts' and no one to wish for this—no one who knew how long they'd stay and no one who thought this was where they would stay. Essa walked the tent rows, shouting, gathering the other mothers and letting them help her carry the child somewhere anywhere, Follow me, and Essa followed, We'll bring her in here with me, and Essa took her there, lay down beside her.

Milde would later understand that she knew the Outskirts by her body even before this had become her wish, and then imagined that it had been her body that wished the place to her; that the night when her body went cold and thereafter let the cold live as a coolness within, was also the same night that the Outskirts formulated itself and rose like a buzz over the wall of mountains.

Milde is seven years old and the winter is cold. She is told that she has been very ill and is only now on the road to recovery. Actually, she knows that she has been ill, but can't remember how long or why. Now that she is better, she sees that the tents and the place are different, Essa is no longer sitting by her alone. Several mothers and several of the children she plays with are huddled in their tent and their tent is full. It is warm and lovely and full in their tent, and she enjoys it so much. Milde tries to sit up. Success, she can sit for a while, talk to the children, drink lukewarm tea. Later, when she needs to rest, the mothers take the children away and leave her alone with Essa. But even Essa is not the same as before. Essa is happy, happier. She holds Milde tight and tells her that everything is going to get better, that she will soon be well and that the moment she is well, she'll get to go back to school. Here, among the tents. Here among the tents, the mothers intend to build a school, Essa tells her, and as soon as Milde is well, she and Essa will help prepare for the first day of school.

What is a home? The Outskirts became Milde's home.

So the deportees settled in the evening light, in the dawn, when the sun was at its highest.

In the morning, the mothers each picked up the largest bucket they could carry and the children each a cup; just as the sun began to warm and a protective mist lay between them and the sun and the children's black hair, the mothers and children walked the tent rows and greeted each other, carried their buckets and cups to the tap and fetched water home.

Later, when Essa had built her home, its walls rising along the grooves in the sheet metal found among the garbage and scraps, Milde would hang drawings everywhere to remind her of what she wished for and liked right then, what was best and most fun and what she wanted to look at and keep close to her.

The homes on the Outskirts would be built just as the first night of frost fell and the soldiers, who'd been waiting to take the mothers and children across the border, simply packed up their tents and left.

The first homes would be built right as the border opened and the machines started running beyond the slope of the Outskirts and the sound of highway construction kept them awake the whole night through.

The soldiers first summoned the mothers and children and gave each mother a document. They said: 'As the border is about to be opened, you no longer need us to escort you.

'However, this does not mean that you'll be given access to your old homes.

'No, as long as your nationality has not been established, it is not possible for you to return to your former place of residence.

'The document also states that you now own these tents and whatever you have so far acquired or borrowed.

'The borrowed items do not need to be returned or paid for, and the items you have otherwise acquired do not need to be accounted for.

'We will also leave behind the stock of goods and tools we have kept in the guard post—these too are now jointly owned by you.

'Beyond this and going forward, we have no other business here—this document tells you everything you need to know about the conditions of your residence here, as well as the contact details of the relevant authorities, should they be needed.

'These documents do in fact require a signature to take effect, but we'll ignore that procedure this time.

'Your signatures simply cannot be verified and therefore are meaningless.

'However, we encourage you to keep the document in case you need to present it at a later time.

'You could, for example, use it as proof of ownership if you ever have to move away from here and want to take the tents with you.

'Or include it in your citizenship application to support your story.

'An application for citizenship is not free of charge and is best done in the city.

'Identification and proof of heritage will be required, and your birth certificate will not be valid as such.

'Nor is this document valid proof of such.

'For those of you who are in possession of both your own and your father's birth certificates, the chances are better, provided that your father was also born in our country.

'The application will still cost money, but with a father's birth certificate, the authorities are more likely to find evidence in support of citizenship in our country.

'In other words, improving your chances with this process.

'For those of you who do not have your father's birth certificate, we can tell you that it is not possible to obtain such a document without identification.

'For those who do not have a registered father, the procedure will be longer and more difficult.

'In any case, you and your children must apply for a residence permit in our country as soon as possible and then make sure to renew your residence permit every three months.

'The residence permit is a limited residence permit until you manage to prove some form of citizenship somewhere.

'If it turns out that you belong to another country, your case will be handled in a certain way.

'If it turns out that you belong to our country, you are our citizens and have the right to reclaim your homes.

'The application is made at the nearest police station and costs a certain amount.

'If you apply only for your children, it will cost more, and if you apply as a family, it will cost less.

'However, applying as a family is not an option for you as you are only mothers and children.

'You must apply within the next three weeks for your situation here to be taken into consideration.

'If you do not apply within the next three weeks, our country will consider you undocumented.

'Is this clear?

'Have you understood what you need to do?'

Milde is seven years old and is sitting with the other children on the slope where the afternoon mist has just settled, making the world dazzling and milky white. Farther away, the mothers stand in a group, talking loudly to the soldiers who are leaving the tents and the mountain. She can't hear what they're saying, but from time to time, she discerns Essa's voice upset and determined. She cannot hear the soldiers' voices at all—it's as if they aren't there or are there but can no longer speak. She turns around to see if they haven't left and sees that the soldiers' mouths are moving, but she can't understand what they're saying. It's as if she has become deaf to their voices or as if their voices have disappeared into the distance between her and them. She doesn't mind, she doesn't care.

It's winter and Milde and the other children sitting on the slope where the tents end are competing to see who can look into the sun the longest without blinking. Diamond, who lives in the tent next to Milde's, keeps blinking and rubbing her eyes. Milde puts a hand on her shoulder and says it's because she's still small. I'm six years old, Diamond says, looking at Milde. Yes, I know, Milde says proudly, but I'll be eight in six months and I know what I'm talking about. None of the children can look into the sun as long as Milde can. She wins every time and then lies down contentedly to rest in the dust. Around this time in the afternoon is the easiest, Milde thinks as she stretches out—at no other time is it as easy to look into the sun as when it's at its biggest and whitest, and has no edges, like now.

What is a home? The Outskirts became Milde's home.

That's how the Outskirts was born and grew—when the soldiers departed something about it cracked open, or rather when the mothers were left on their own there, they saw the place for what it was: a home.

Soon thereafter, the mothers made their way down the slope and walked in all directions—towards the sugarcane fields to ask the sugarcane farmers for food and work and into the caves to see if the caves offered shelter and coolness.

The mothers walked behind the gas stations and found a piece of scrap metal, then up to the whitewashed houses to pick raspberries, plums and as many cherries as they could get their hands on from the gardens; they climbed gates to peer into the houses closest to the sugarcane fields and pinched fruit from the roadside greengrocer.

Later, the mothers went all the way to the city to demand food and money from the city and at first didn't know how to find their way back there, back into the city but back to where? Back into the city that was as familiar as a body part—hands, voice or stomach—but *which* hands now grown bigger and stronger, and *which* voice broken, hoarse and different?

The mothers entered the city and immediately made their way to the sea, walked with their pants rolled up into the same water that they had not longed for all the while they'd been living in the city and let the sand wash in and out between their toes and over their ankles, cracked from impact and cold. The mothers let the water rise up their calves and stood with their shirts unbuttoned and their hair loose in the afternoon sun white and swollen, closed their eyes and listened to the sea, and only turned around when the person watching over the beach called out to them and asked them to leave. Suddenly, remembering why they'd never wanted to come here before, the mothers slowly approached the man, ruddy and round, and asked: What do you pay for beach cleanup?

Soon the mothers were carrying metal sheet after metal sheet on their back up the slope and into the tents, and soon they were nailing wood and plastic to seal the gaps in their homes.

Soon the houses of the Outskirts were rattling and crowding, the ditch rippling before them, and soon the children were walking along the pathway marbled by rain-dissolved cardboard that protected their feet and marked the way home.

With each passing day, the mothers of the Outskirts found more and more to carry with them, and one day came up the slope with a stool to put against the wall and, on another day, porcelain bowls a sugarcane farmer had wanted to get rid of; the mothers filled their bags with old toys for the children to play with and carried home torn sweaters, shirts and pants and refashioned them.

Later, when the uprising was being planned, the mothers and children of the Outskirts would clear away what was in their homes and lift up the metal floors. They would dig as deep as they could before reaching bedrock and first fill one pit with gas canisters and then the other pit with gunpowder.

It happened one day that an excavator and two vans drove halfway up the slope and in front of the mountain where the mountain flattened out—as the mountain one day had flattened out into a steppe for the mothers and children who would later build the Outskirts and make it their home.

The children who saw the vehicles driving up would run to and from the site and tell their mothers the latest news, Now they've dug a wide pit but not very deep, and now they've put up fences and left the excavator behind.

The men who'd driven up the slope would one day approach the children sitting next to the fence and ask them to leave, to go home. The children then moved to a spot not far away and sat down, made piles of gravel and pebbles and eventually heard a sound they couldn't place and after that a blast as if the mountain were splitting in two. Soon thereafter, when the blasting in the mountain made it seem as if it were going to collapse, the children dust-covered would run home to the Outskirts and tell their mothers what had happened.

There was blasting in the mountain once and then many times more in the following days; the piles of gravel and pebbles were levelled to the ground and the dust rose as if in waves, pushing up against the mist and sinking back; the walls and roofs of the Outskirts collapsed in on each other and the children rubbed their eyes, now scratched by dust and pebbles.

Two days later, the pit received its first big load of garbage and was thereafter filled up every week with load upon load, eventually the dump itself rose like a mountain within the mountain, drawing the mothers and children to it.

Milde is ten years old and afraid of the men who have appeared. The hair she has always preferred to cut off has again grown large and for once she no longer wants to get rid of it. This makes Essa happy and excited. I can braid it for you, Essa says, twisting her hair carefully against her scalp and doing it up nicely. They sit in the shade among the other mothers and children and talk about the excavator on the other side of the mountain. At the end of each braid, Essa attaches a bright plastic bead that will later shine against Milde's nape smooth and thin. Essa manages to get half her hair done before the first blast, and the mothers throw themselves over the children and hold them close. The mothers and children of the Outskirts watch the walls collapse in on each other and the tarpaulins fall—they see the cats running between the metal walls and the school shed shaking.

Later that night, Essa dresses all in black and takes Milde with half her hair undone to the slope where some of the mothers and children are sitting, asks her to wait there. Essa goes with two other mothers to the place where Milde knows the hole is being blasted and disappears in the dark. When Essa returns, she is covered in dust and enlivened. Milde recognizes her by her shirt and the energy in her voice, even though Essa has forgotten to take off the shawl hiding her face. At dawn the next morning, Milde carefully leaves her home and goes to where the hole is, and sees that all the fences have been torn down and the excavator that scraped the bedrock bare is overturned, its windows smashed on all sides.

What is a home? The Outskirts is my home, Milde would say.

One day the mothers and children of the Outskirts would put three empty tents side by side and tear out the walls between them, saying this is the Outskirts' school.

In the tent the mothers and children would hang red, green and yellow tin lids as decoration, and proudly say: This is our school and our meeting place—here the children will be during the day and in the evenings we too, here the children will learn about the world and in the evenings we too, with some tea and some milk and some honey, each with a sheet of paper and a pencil and a book under their arm that we've read together and will discuss.

The mothers and children of the Outskirts would enter the school shed one by one and hang photographs of all their role models on the school walls. Once a month they would decide on a book to read aloud, and in the afternoons gather on the slope of the Outskirts with sugared tea in jugs and bread and butter in bowls.

Later, the Outskirts would build a school shed twice as big and leave a piece of the now-demolished school tent hanging from the roof, making its presence felt every time someone slammed the metal door behind them or when Essa eagerly wrote on the slate cracked from edge to edge.

Essa wrote: For whom? and said it was the most important question to ask. Ask each and every person. Ask it of those who assert something is good, right and correct, and of those who label something as bad, dangerous or forbidden. Ask it of your siblings and your mothers and your friends when your siblings and your mothers and your friends are unclear for whom. Ask it of me when I assert something without explaining myself, and ask it of yourselves each time you wish for something but don't know if your wish is the right one. Ask it, and then let the answer guide you home.

It happened that the school was given old textbooks from that nice lady in the nearest library about an hour's walk away from the slope. The children and mothers of the Outskirts were among the library's most dedicated borrowers, and the nice librarian couldn't help but think of them from time to time—their zeal as readers and their politeness—and from time to time wished they'd visit with their interest and earnest love of books.

Cracked at the spine and with pages torn away here and there, These books are going to be tossed out anyway, she said, But I put them aside for you to look at. Essa, never as happy as when she was given books, would approach the stack smiling wide.

Essa and the ten children and mothers of the Outskirts who on this occasion had been able to come along to the library would say thank you very much and tell that nice librarian she was always welcome to put books aside for them, I find it very hard to imagine that we'd say no to any book, Essa would say, thinking that a white lie was no lie at all and that white lies rarely cause any harm. She could always use the worst books as a cautionary tale, and if they were too bad even for that, they could either be sold at market or be used as trivets for the pots and pans of the Outskirts.

She thought that ending up a trivet was a fine and most honourable fate for a bad book that would otherwise be burned, and just as Essa couldn't imagine what it was like to be surrounded by thousands upon thousands of books every day, the nice librarian could not imagine Essa and the Outskirts' lack and why someone would choose to make a trivet out of a book just to be close to the essence of a book rather than sell the book at market and get a few extra coins.

They'll always come in handy, Essa would say with a smile, and that nice librarian would slide the tattered books across the circulation desk and shake Essa's hand.

What is a home? The Outskirts is my home, Milde would say.

It was here that it all began—from the school shed onwards, the Outskirts grew and grew.

The children of the Outskirts got used to sharing what was available in the school shed and to economizing with pencils, erasers and paper. They spent the first day of school breaking the pencils in half and cutting each eraser into three equal pieces. They folded each sheet of paper in half to make a writing pad and Essa would help them to carefully write their names on the front. Then Essa took out powdered turmeric and the bowl of dried beets that she'd soaked the night before and let the children, now lining up at her desk, paint the paper with gentle strokes of a thick brush, soon filling it with pink, yellow and white. She also took out the desert flowers that she'd dried over the summer in the depths of her library books and scattered them across the corrugated metal floor for the children to choose from. Take one, and if there are any left over, feel free to take another.

Essa, who made sure that the most essential items in the school shed were available, let the first day of school be easy and tried not to worry about everything they didn't have right then and wouldn't get, not the way their economy was looking. It was only later—when Milde decided to travel all the way up to the black hole the Mass in order to write from there at length and for a long time to the Outskirts and made it one of her many conditions that every school year the Department of Education should supply the Outskirts with books, paper, pencils and erasers—that this need was met.

Essa, who'd never before had so many materials and supplies at her disposal when teaching, would for the first few years readily accept the packages sent to the slope and carried all the way up. She'd take pleasure in science and mathematics, make use of the world map and the art book and delight a great many times in the grammar exercises she outlined on the board and slowly went through.

How important is it to write like that, the children would ask, and Essa would answer: It's not as important as not writing like that if you don't want to.

Milde is fifteen years old and high summer is endless. Three days a week she does her rounds on the beach with a broken cooler over her arm, and on the remaining days she sits in the school shed reading and writing with the younger children. Like the other mothers and children, she also goes to the slope on afternoons when she is at home in her Outskirts and listens with a cup of tea in her hand to the reading-aloud session, which they all look forward to.

The soft drinks don't get cold, she knows this—the heavy cooler is mostly for show and has long since stopped having any effect. When the white tourists call out to her, they first ask for a can and then a different one. None of these are cold, they say. Sure they are, says Milde, here, feel them. When the white tourists are once again holding a soft-drink can, Milde gives their children a wink. The children jump into their mothers' arms, not taking their eyes off Milde, clutching their cuddly toy. No, they're not even a bit cold, we don't want any, the mothers say, returning the can once more. Milde adjusts her sun visor, picks up the bag from the sand and walks away. Behind her, the children start crying and the mothers comfort them. The children do indeed want a soft drink, and it doesn't matter that it's warm. The mothers try to convince them that they'll get a cold soft drink as soon as they leave the beach, and it will be much tastier and lovelier, but the children keep crying and wanting. Milde moves farther and farther away. Suddenly the mothers call Milde back. Hey, you, come here. Now the fathers have also woken up, are looking around, What's going on? He wants a soft drink, the mothers say, taking out money. But is it cold? No. Then why are you buying it? He wants a soft drink, the mothers say again, searching their handbag. The children cry louder and louder, and the beach slowly empties of people, the afternoon sun spreads white and big, and in the Outskirts the children leave the school shed and move towards the slope to play. The fathers look at Milde. She looks away, at the sea, again takes out the soft drink and looks at the child who immediately puts the can to his mouth, takes her money and leaves.

Later, just as the summer season ends, Milde helps Essa prepare for the first day of school. There aren't many first graders, but they're extremely cute, and she wants nothing more than to help them settle in. She brings in several bundles of paper and a box of pencils and erasers, wipes the metal floor with a rag and straightens the portraits on the walls. Milde pulls out a bag of shells that she has collected during her rounds on the beach and scatters them next to Essa's desert flowers. She watches the children carefully select a single bloom to press into the palm of their hand and tells them this isn't necessary, they can choose as many as they like, what's important is that they only choose the ones they really like and not take more just because they can. And the children once again hover over the pile and attentively search for more.

What is a home? The Outskirts is my home, Milde would say.

It was in the school shed that the children sat, and later their mothers too, in the evenings every evening, in the evenings every evening to talk about the week just gone and the week to come, and to talk about the garbage, the sugarcane, the bicycle and the boardwalk. It was also in the school shed that they would later all crowd while planning the uprising and everything that would make the uprising work was taken care of. Everyone saw the questions forming on the blackboard and those who step by step had learned to read raised their hands, spoke their piece.

In preparation for the uprising, which lasted two days and two nights, the children of the Outskirts would sleep in two-hour shifts and learn how to keep watch while playing in their waking hours. Drowsy but awake, the children would first run along the slope to spy across the road where it was lined with gas stations and dark cafés, and after that up the mountain where the mountain overlooked the highway and the desert vast and pink.

The children spread out and squatted in the dust, whistling one time for arrivals and three times for danger.

They whistled and waited and then changed as the mothers, dressed in black and silent, crept forward to take over, to offer food and warm clothes, and ran a smooth hand over the children's faces, accompanying them home.

When Milde, Diamond and Trinidad walked up the slope to the Outskirts at dawn, when everyone was waiting for them, and the children who'd been keeping watch along the mountain saw them coming like three shadows sweeping across the ground and vanishing, the Outskirts understood a new era had begun.

There and then, the new era had begun, and perhaps never to end hereafter.

At the sight of the shadows, the children ran along the ditch to Essa, bent over her writing board—the paper still white and blank and the pencil still sharp, a nub of an eraser beside it. The children ran to Essa and after that didn't have to say anything and so didn't say anything at all—Essa got up, wrapped her shawl around her shoulders and followed the children outside.

The mothers and children of the Outskirts understood that it was only for them that the three daughters had carried out what in the city was called an insult but in the Outskirts was considered a sigh of relief and an uprising, no more and no less. A sigh of relief long delayed and nigh on stillborn were it not for this particular moment and these particular three who'd both spoken and taken action, not just spoken and dreamed—who'd both spoken and taken action and who now also had it in them to come home in something other than a body bag, thank God.

They were the ones who'd brought the new era with them, and it was with them that the Outskirts now wanted to celebrate.

The mothers of the Outskirts stripped Milde, Trinidad and Diamond of their clothes, shoes and bags and threw everything into the fire on the upturned car hood in the centre of the Outskirts. The mothers gave each of the three her own bar of store-bought soap and each her own bottle of hair dye and told them not to stop washing until the soap was all gone and the smell of ammonia had set in as it should.

After that, they dressed their daughters and led them into the school shed, where jasmine flowers garlanded the walls and ceiling. Milde would later often think about that meal the Outskirts had arranged and how it had all come to pass. She'd wonder again and again how the mothers had managed to stash so many goodies in their midst and how long it must have taken them to cook everything. Later, once they'd finished eating, Essa stood up and said that it was now time for them to be off. For a few months only and no longer, Milde would be away. For a few months, just until everything calmed down and no one bothered anymore to look for the girl who'd been spotted at the site and who now was wanted.

The uprising set every tourist's car in motion, emptied the city's beach loungers and left the smell of smoke hanging over the outdoor cafés, as if each chair and each tablecloth were occupied by what had just taken place. Where the smoke had rolled in—across the polished marble paving that had been laid in recent years so the city would look like other tourist towns and would welcome those who ambled through places where things could cost what they might so long as there was a safe distance between them and the cobbled streets of the old neighborhoods and the condemned wooden and limestone buildings—a pillar now rose into the air, swaying to and fro above the restaurants, to and fro and undulating above the outdoor seating, and slowly the smoke, like fog, rolled across the marble paving still smooth and cool but changed, isn't that right?

Sure, the marble floor still shone as if it had not one scratch or hole, and yet it seemed as if the surface had suddenly become lacklustre and not as pleasing to pattering shoes. Yes, after the uprising, the marble paving in the city would never again be as pleasing for tourists to patter along and never again as bright, hard and shiny as the city wanted it to be. Something had changed and this was a change Milde wanted.

Yes, this is how I want it to feel, Milde thought at dawn as she stood holding a lit Molotov cocktail in her hand and sent it shattering through the top-floor windows of the city planning office—this is how I want it to go.

Milde is seventeen years old. Diamond is sixteen years old. Trinidad is twenty years old.

Milde watches the smoke swirl through the trees and swallow the canopy whole. The birds, whose deafening chirrup had filled her ears, now flee—around and around the canopy, the rising birds flee, around and around the smoke that's taking them in and out of darkness. It's much bigger than she'd imagined, the smoke. It flows, billows and flows even more; it swirls, rushes forth and stings her eyes. Diamond and Trinidad hiss from behind the bushes that they have to go now, come on Milde, we have to go now, hurry up. Milde hears them and knows they have to go, of course they do, but she can't budge. Everything is so much bigger and darker than she'd imagined—everything so much clearer than she'd dared hope. It's as if the day has never been anything but pallor, and the night has never been anything but this black smoke that rolls in and spreads large and heavy across this place. Milde doesn't like the day and how it makes her appear—she only likes the night and the starry sky at night and mostly wishes there had never been anything other than night into which to sink. And now—here it is: the

Outskirts' homemade night, dark and striking. She can't possibly walk away from it just like that, not now, not until the black has played and flowed a little more and the image of everything they're doing has been etched firmly on her chest and behind her eyelids.

Suddenly she is knocked to the ground, can't breathe.

Someone lies on top of Milde and pushes her slim body to the ground, pins her hands behind her back and drags her away from all the smoke. She can't breathe for the pressure on her chest and tries to lift her face from the grass, to say something. He bats her around more and then harder, searches her body for weapons and finally turns her around, rips off her hood. He stares, stunned. He doesn't really know what he's looking at and so involuntarily loosens his grip, doesn't seem to believe that she's the one who set the fire and looks around for someone else. All is chirping birds and all chirping stops when Trinidad fires her rifle into the air—all is day and the whole day is obscured as the guard releases Milde's hands so he can shield his body. Milde tears herself free and crawls as if stabbed in the gut towards the bushes where she knows Trinidad and Diamond are waiting. They run up to Milde, take her by the arms, and together they vanish.

BALSAM KARAM (b. 1983) is of Kurdish ancestry and has lived in Sweden since she was a young child. She is an author, librarian, and university lecturer, and made her literary debut in 2018 with the critically acclaimed *Event Horizon*, which was shortlisted for the Katapult Prize. Her second novel, *The Singularity*, was published in Sweden in 2021 and was shortlisted for the August Prize.

SASKIA VOGEL is the author of *Permission* and the translator of over twenty Swedish-language books. She was awarded the Berlin Senate Endowment for Non-German Literature and was a finalist for the National Book Award. From Los Angeles, she now lives in Berlin.

The Feminist Press publishes books that ignite movements and social transformation. Celebrating our legacy, we lift up insurgent and marginalized voices from around the world to build a more just future.

See our complete list of books at **feministpress.org**